THE HALF-CASTE

broadview editions
series editor: Martin R. Boyne

He leaped in at the chamber window, and angrily asked
me by what right I interfered.

PAGE 49.

Frontispiece from *The Half-Caste: An Old Governess's Tale* (W. & R. Chambers, 1897).

THE HALF-CASTE

Dinah Mulock Craik

edited by
Melissa Edmundson

broadview editions

BROADVIEW PRESS – www.broadviewpress.com
Peterborough, Ontario, Canada

Founded in 1985, Broadview Press remains a wholly independent publishing house. Broadview's focus is on academic publishing; our titles are accessible to university and college students as well as scholars and general readers. With over 600 titles in print, Broadview has become a leading international publisher in the humanities, with world-wide distribution. Broadview is committed to environmentally responsible publishing and fair business practices.

The interior of this book is printed on 100% recycled paper.

Library and Archives Canada Cataloguing in Publication

Craik, Dinah Maria Mulock, 1826–1887, author
The half-caste / Dinah Mulock Craik ; edited by Melissa Edmundson.

(Broadview editions)
Includes bibliographical references.
ISBN 978-1-55481-275-2 (paperback)

1. Young women—Fiction. 2. Racially mixed people—Fiction. 3. England—Fiction. 4. Domestic fiction. 5. Bildungsromans. I. Edmundson, Melissa, editor II. Title. III. Series: Broadview editions

PR4516.H34 2016 823'.8 C2016-903441-0

Broadview Editions
The Broadview Editions series is an effort to represent the ever-evolving canon of texts in the disciplines of literary studies, history, philosophy, and political theory. A distinguishing feature of the series is the inclusion of primary source documents contemporaneous with the work.

Advisory editor for this volume: Michel Pharand

Broadview Press handles its own distribution in North America
PO Box 1243, Peterborough, Ontario K9J 7H5, Canada
555 Riverwalk Parkway, Tonawanda, NY 14150, USA
Tel: (705) 743-8990; Fax: (705) 743-8353
email: customerservice@broadviewpress.com

Distribution is handled by Eurospan Group in the UK, Europe, Central Asia, Middle East, Africa, India, Southeast Asia, Central America, South America, and the Caribbean. Distribution is handled by Footprint Books in Australia and New Zealand.

Broadview Press acknowledges the financial support of the Government of Canada through the Canada Book Fund for our publishing activities.

Typesetting and assembly: True to Type Inc., Claremont, Canada
Cover Design: Aldo Fierro

PRINTED IN CANADA

Contents

Acknowledgements

I am grateful to Don LePan of Broadview Press for his early support of this project, as well as to Marjorie Mather for her help in shepherding this book through the publication process. My thanks go as well to Broadview Editions series editor Martin Boyne and advisory editor Michel Pharand for their careful reading of the entire manuscript and their many helpful comments and suggestions. I would also like to thank Jeffrey Makala for his editorial assistance throughout the creation of this edition.

Introduction

Dinah Mulock Craik (1826–87) was one of the best-selling authors of the nineteenth century. In a career that spanned forty years, she published numerous novels, children's books, essays, poetry, and translations. People made pilgrimages to her London residence in order to meet the famed "authoress of *John Halifax*." She was awarded a Civil List pension in 1864, one of the few awards given to British writers at the time. Upon her death in 1887, numerous obituaries and memorials in both Britain and North America paid tribute to Craik's life and work. She was the quintessential Victorian woman writer: her character calm and unassuming, her works sentimental and instructive. Because of this conservative portrayal, Craik's status as an author quickly passed from public and critical notice, and she was largely forgotten for much of the twentieth century.[1]

However, a 1975 essay by Elaine Showalter reintroduced the author to a modern audience. Showalter identifies Craik as part of the "second wave of Victorian women novelists" who were traditionally not "taken seriously" by literary critics.[2] As a defense against this critical negligence, Showalter discusses the ways in which Craik's novels were an often subversive space for unresolved or conflicted emotions for Victorian women writers. She writes that Craik "excelled at the peculiar combination of didacticism and subversive feminism, which at much more developed levels of intellect, characterized the novels of Charlotte Brontë and George Eliot."[3] Craik's life and work received extended treatment in Sally Mitchell's *Dinah Mulock Craik* (1983), which

---

1 Though Dinah Mulock Craik did not marry until 1865, and therefore published much of her writing (including *The Half-Caste*) under her maiden name, I refer to her throughout this Introduction as "Craik" for consistency.

2 Elaine Showalter, "Dinah Mulock Craik and the Tactics of Sentiment: A Case Study in Victorian Female Authorship," *Feminist Studies* 2 (1975): 5.

3 Showalter 6. Charlotte Brontë (1816–55) was a novelist best known for *Jane Eyre* (1847), *Shirley* (1849), and *Villette* (1853). George Eliot (1819–80) was the pen name of novelist Mary Ann (or Marian) Evans, who wrote *Adam Bede* (1859), *The Mill on the Floss* (1860), *Silas Marner* (1861), *Romola* (1863), *Middlemarch* (1871–72), and *Daniel Deronda* (1876).

documents the author's public and private life, the success of *John Halifax, Gentleman* (1856), her work in children's literature, her role as a woman novelist, and her place in the feminist tradition. Thirty years after Mitchell's pioneering work, Craik became the subject of a special issue of *Women's Writing* dedicated to the continued recovery and reassessment of her work. Introducing the issue, Karen Bourrier describes the prospective avenues for future Craik studies, from the careers of Victorian women writers and children's literature, to disability and postcolonial studies.[1] It is within the latter area that this Broadview edition situates Craik's work, both in how she responds to prevailing cultural and racial attitudes of her time and in how her novella can broaden our understanding of Victorian women's interpretation of empire within the context of mixed-race and postcolonial studies.

The Eurasian Community

In order to understand the cultural importance of *The Half-Caste*, readers need to consider Craik's work within the wider context of nineteenth-century understandings of the mixed-race "Eurasian" community in India. During the eighteenth century, members of this group enjoyed more social privilege because the British East India Company[2] allowed relationships between its British employees and high-caste Indian women.[3] It was thought at the time

1 Karen Bourrier, "Introduction: Rereading Dinah Mulock Craik," *Women's Writing* 20.3 (2013): 287–96.

2 The British East India Company was founded by Queen Elizabeth I's royal charter on 31 December 1600 in order to secure access to the lucrative East Indian spice trade. Originally controlled by shareholders and managed by a group of directors, the Company increasingly fell under parliamentary control in the second half of the eighteenth century. The East India Company Act of 1773 created the position of Governor General of India, first held by Warren Hastings (1732–1818). A series of Charter Acts in 1813, 1833, and 1853 also ensured greater government control over the Company. The Company was subsequently blamed for much of the administrative mismanagement that led to the Indian Uprising of 1857 (also called the First War of Indian Independence), and the following year, the British Crown assumed direct rule of the Indian subcontinent. In 1873, Queen Victoria was named Empress of India and the East India Company was officially disbanded. The period of British control of India, which began in 1858 and lasted until Indian independence in 1947, is commonly referred to as the British Raj (or British "rule").

3 For a discussion of the varieties of relationships among British men and Indian women, including the marriage between James Achilles Kirk-

that the children of these unions would cement Indo-British ties, being symbolic of a larger "marriage" between the two cultures. As the British missionary presence increased during the early decades of the nineteenth century, accompanied by greater numbers of British women traveling to India, a stricter moral code took hold. Consequently, unions between British men and Indian women were increasingly disparaged. In addition to the questions of morality that were attached to these relationships, a political need to distance the colonizing British from the colonized Indians emerged. In order to maintain control of its massive territory and the millions of Indian people within its borders, the British had to continuously display their cultural and racial dominance. During the second half of the nineteenth century, racial boundaries became even more defined, and distinct racial hierarchies helped Great Britain forward the myth of its superiority. In her discussion of Victorians and race, Christine Bolt sees this distinction as the shift from a concept of race viewed solely through a biological lens to one also viewed through a cultural lens:

> If all could agree that anthropology was the science of man, the proper methods of anthropologists, however, aroused considerable disagreement. Both cultural characteristics, such as language, and physical features were used to classify the different divisions of man. Ultimately the two became confused, so that something called "race" came to be seen as the prime determinant of all the important traits of body and soul, character and personality, of human beings and nations. In other

---

patrick (1764–1805), an officer in the British East India Company's army, and the Indian noblewoman Khair un-Nissa (d. 1813), see William Dalrymple's *White Mughals: Love and Betrayal in Eighteenth-Century India* (London: HarperCollins, 2002). In India, the caste system is a class-based hierarchy within the Hindu religion and governs social interactions. One is born into a "varna" (class), with Brahmins being the highest and Shudras the lowest. The so-called "untouchables" are considered to be beneath the Shudra class. The caste system also dictates the organization of labor. Brahmins are the most educated and influential citizens, while members of the Shudra class are largely employed as semi-skilled or unskilled workers. The caste system became more prevalent during the years of British rule in India, when Indians were employed in government administration based on their caste. Indian women who entered relationships with British men were described as forfeiting their caste status.

words, race became far more than a biological concept: race and culture were dangerously linked.[1]

Likewise, Kenneth Ballhatchet has commented that "English class attitudes are transformed into racial attitudes in an imperial setting."[2] This progression of race viewed from an anthropological basis to something cultural or class-driven is an important shift from the more ambivalent idea of "empire" to the negative conception of "imperialism."[3] In order to maintain the colonial system, the British had to deny any biological connection they had with their Indian "subjects." This meant that, as a cultural group, Eurasians were ostracized from the civil, military, and social worlds that increasingly made up the British Raj.

Eurasians themselves were quite aware of their unequal status. During the 1820s, they called for greater social, political, and financial equality. In 1830, the East Indians' Petition was presented to Parliament by John William Ricketts (1791–1835), a prominent civil servant and son of an English father and an Indian mother.[4] In the petition, a majority of the educated Eurasians in Calcutta formally requested that they be granted full legal status as British subjects. They also asked for increased opportunities as civil servants in India, an opportunity, they argued, that would save the British money because civil servants would not need to be imported from England (134, 135). Much like a previous petition made in 1818, the new petition was unsuccessful and did little to influence the way in which Eurasians were treated within the colonial system. According to Hawes, the Petition of 1830 marked a new era in which Eurasians had to increasingly fight for

1 Christine Bolt, *Victorian Attitudes to Race* (London: Routledge and Kegan Paul, 1971), 9.

2 Kenneth Ballhatchet, *Race, Sex and Class under the Raj: Imperial Attitudes and Policies and Their Critics, 1793–1905* (New York: St. Martin's P, 1980), 121.

3 The term "empire" generally denotes a more benign period of commercial control over India, roughly spanning the eighteenth century until 1870. The more detrimental idea of "imperialism" is used to describe the increasingly oppressive nature of British Crown rule over the people of the Indian subcontinent, from approximately 1870 until Indian independence in 1947.

4 Christopher J. Hawes, *Poor Relations: The Making of a British Community in British India, 1773–1833* (Richmond, UK: Curzon, 1996), 91. Subsequent references to this source will appear parenthetically within the text.

opportunities among a growing population of British émigrés (149). The Eurasians' call for equality and increased opportunities was echoed in 1825 by an anonymous writer in the *Asiatic Journal*, who proclaimed, "There can be no doubt that they [Eurasians] are entitled to all the civil privileges and functions of both parents."[1]

The difficulties Eurasians faced regarding identity and social acceptance extended into the actual naming of the cultural group. According to Hawes, as early as 1818 a petition was made to Lord Hastings in Calcutta to use "Eurasian" instead of "half-caste" in official documents, and in 1827 two hundred Eurasians petitioned British officials in Madras to end the use of "half-caste" in government documents. During the same period, other names for the community were suggested, including "Anglo-Asian," "Indo-Briton," and "East Indian," but "Eurasian" remained the most widely used for the rest of the nineteenth century (89).[2] Despite efforts to give the community an acceptable name, social prejudice continued. As late as 1914, *The Century Dictionary* included the following definition for "Eurasian," which, far from helping to "define" the group, only advanced stereotypes: "A half-caste, one of whose parents is European, or of pure European descent, and the other Asiatic: originally restricted to one born in Hindustan of a Hindu mother and a European (especially a Portuguese) father, but now applied to all half-breeds of mixed Asiatic and European blood, and their offspring. Also called *chee-chee*."[3] The Victorian obsession with

1 "On the Policy of the British Government towards the Indo-Britons," *Asiatic Journal* 20 (September 1825): 307.

2 By 1910, Eurasians had adopted the term "Anglo-Indian," a description that had previously been used to describe the British domiciled in India. In the 1911 census, the Government of British India officially replaced "Eurasian" with "Anglo-Indian" as the term used to describe people of mixed white and Asian ethnicity. In this Introduction, I use "Eurasian" to refer to people of mixed race living in India, and "Anglo-Indian" to refer to British residents in India.

3 "Eurasian," *The Century Dictionary: An Encyclopedic Lexicon of the English Language*, vol. 2 (New York: The Century Company, 1914). "Chee-chee" (also referred to as "chi chi") was a local dialect prevalent in Eurasian communities. The fear of developing the accent was one of several reasons why the British found it necessary to send their children back to England at an early age. *Hobson-Jobson: A Glossary of Colloquial Anglo-Indian Words and Phrases* (London: J. Murray, 1903) gives the following definition: "CHEECHEE, adj. A disparaging term (*continued*)

classification likewise extended to this mixed-race group. By 1886, *The Anglo-Indian* was proposing the following racial identification system: "Anglo-Indian" meant "those who have either no or very slight admixture with the native races"; "Eurasians" were "those in whom the European and native descent are more evenly balanced"; and "East Indians" were "those of remote European descent and approaching more closely to the native type."[1] The frequent use of hyphenated names to describe this cultural community points as well to the protean qualities of hybridity, with its continuous blending of various identities and cultures. Robert J.C. Young discusses hybridity in terms of ethnic and cultural "grafting," while he also notices that, as a nineteenth-century term, hybridity, once used to denote "a physiological phenomenon," now has various cultural connotations and political implications when it is applied to the relationship between imperial nations and colonial/postcolonial communities.[2] Young cites Gargi Bhattacharyya's assertion that "in terms of power relations there is no difference between [the terms] 'British' and 'English,'"[3] a notion that further indicates the fluidity of both national and ethnic identity and calls attention to the necessarily constrictive use of labels and cultural classification systems.

Some commentators sought to raise awareness of the prejudices against Eurasians, but these voices represented a minority

---

applied to half-castes or Eurasians ... and also to their manner of speech. The word is said to be taken from *chī* (Fie!), a common native (S. Indian) interjection of remonstrance or reproof, supposed to be much used by the class in question.... It should, however, be added that there are many well-educated East Indians who are quite free from this mincing accent" (186). In *Memoirs of a Griffin; Or, A Cadet's First Year in India* (1880, new ed.), Captain Francis J. Bellew recalled the accent as "a singular variety of the Anglo-Saxon tongue called the *Cheechee* language (Hindustanee idiom Englished), then new to me—a dialect which constitutes a distinguishing mark of those born and bred in India, and the leading peculiarity of which consists in laying a false emphasis, particularly on such small words as *to*, *me*, *and*, &c." (91).

1 *The Anglo-Indian* (9 January 1886): 19. Quoted in Indrani Sen, *Woman and Empire: Representations in the Writings of British India, 1858–1900* (Hyderabad: Orient Longman, 2002), 49, n. 38. Subsequent references to *Woman and Empire* will appear parenthetically within the text.

2 Robert J.C. Young, *Colonial Desire: Hybridity in Theory, Culture and Race* (London: Routledge, 1995), 6.

3 Cited in Young 3.

of public opinion. Graham Sandberg's "Our Outcast Cousins in India," published in *The Contemporary Review* (1892), discusses the marginal status of the Eurasian: "In the politest parlance, and by themselves, the strange race are denominated *Europeans*; officially they are termed *East Indians*; in general they are spoken of as *Eurasians*; while the genus Snob, unhappily now so plenteous in India, delight to apply such names as 'half-caste,' and even 'darky,' to folk at least superior to themselves."[1] According to Sandberg, this marginality bars the group from being completely accepted by either the British or the Indians: "being wholly neither of one nor of the other, they bear the disabilities of both" (882). Though he urges his readers to recognize this racial inequality, Sandberg's answer to the question of why poverty exists among the group relies on the very same prejudicial judgments that he complains of in the opening paragraphs of the essay: "First, let it be known, there are a want of energy and an hereditary languor which have become almost a disease in the half-caste. Secondly, they have not, of a surety, either the physical strength or the stamina to encounter unremitting manual toil day after day beneath a tropical sun, such as the Hindu lower classes readily undertake" (895). Sandberg then states that the general problem of debt among the group is owing to their refusal to do manual or domestic labor, thus forwarding another pervasive myth of the Eurasian character. Through these contemporary discussions of biracial identity and the Eurasian community, it becomes clear that *The Half-Caste* and the issues it examines are part of a much larger debate centered on the cultural acceptance of this community within British society, both in India and in Britain.

Colonial Anxieties and the Eurasian Woman

As Victorian morals took hold in India—helped by the increased presence of British women on the subcontinent—the practice of British men keeping Indian mistresses decreased. As the nineteenth century progressed, these unions became even more illicit

---

1 Graham Sandberg, "Our Outcast Cousins in India," *Contemporary Review* 61 (June 1892): 880 (italics in original). See Appendix B4. Subsequent references to this source will appear parenthetically within the text.

as Britain sought to maintain a sense of moral and physical superiority over the Indian population. To the British way of thinking, separation was the best way of achieving such imperial ascendency. With increasing British anxieties over the ideas of Darwinian evolution and racial degeneration, relationships between Indians and the British seemingly became a threat to the strength and well-being of British minds and bodies, and thus to the strength and well-being of the empire as a whole.[1] This emphasis on the consequences of contact with the colonial body took on increased focus as the century progressed (and as British cultural attitudes to colonized people simultaneously regressed).[2]

Shompa Lahiri identifies a "biological determinism" that predominated racial understanding in the second half of the nineteenth century and into the twentieth. In much of Anglo-Indian literature, Indians living in England inevitably "reverted to racial type," and "any attempt to challenge essentialism by defying rigidly imposed categories produces discord and ultimate

---

1 The threat of degeneration was a particular concern during the nineteenth century. Arising out of the theories of natural selection and evolution introduced into British culture after the publication of Charles Darwin's (1809–82) *On the Origin of Species* (1859), theories of degeneration suggested that if human beings were capable of evolution, they were also capable of devolution. Further debates about human origins, the existence of an Anglo-Saxon ethnic superiority, and perceived biological dangers brought about by interracial procreation were found in works such as Robert Knox's (1791–1862) *The Races of Men* (1850), Arthur de Gobineau's (1816–82) *Essay on The Inequality of the Human Races* (1855), and Bénédict Morel's (1809–73) *Treatise on Degeneration* (1857). What is now known as "Social Darwinism," which applied biological theories to social behavior, was also forwarded in Cesare Lombroso's (1835–1909) *Criminal Man* (1876) and Max Nordau's (1849–1923) *Degeneration* (1892). These works helped to foster anxiety attached to societal fears over increased populations of foreign-born people within Britain and rising crime rates within increasingly overpopulated British cities.

2 For more on the political implications of such cross-cultural unions, see Nancy L. Paxton, *Writing under the Raj: Gender, Race, and Rape in the British Colonial Imagination, 1830–1947* (New Brunswick, NJ, and London: Rutgers UP, 1999), Durba Ghosh, *Sex and the Family in Colonial India: The Making of Empire* (Cambridge and New York: Cambridge UP, 2006), and Shuchi Kapila, *Educating Seeta: The Anglo-Indian Family Romance and the Poetics of Indirect Rule* (Columbus: Ohio State UP, 2010).

tragedy."[1] Likewise, Phillip Darby claims that Anglo-Indian fiction "takes personal relationships as its point of reference—which is to say that political issues are broached through the depiction of personal feelings and behaviour."[2] Anglo-Indian popular fiction was integral to shaping the British public's conception of race relationships with those they colonized. Darby claims, "For the British there was a sense of vulnerability and a determination to shore up the foundations of power, and hence strict limits to the extent the two peoples could relate" (82). In order to "shore up" this power, British novelists typically emphasized stability over reform and "social distance between ruler and ruled" (90). Consequently, "the fiction of the period marginalized and depersonalized the colonial subject" (90). As this theory certainly holds true for the majority of Anglo-Indian literature and its depictions of Indian and biracial characters, Dinah Mulock Craik's *The Half-Caste*, with its portrayal of Zillah Le Poer, stands as an important exception.

In recent years, scholars have attempted to uncover the extent to which race and empire influenced women's thinking and writing in the nineteenth century.[3] What was for many years thought to be

---

1 Shompa Lahiri, *Indians in Britain: Anglo-Indian Encounters, Race and Identity, 1880–1930* (London and Portland, OR: Frank Cass, 2000), 103.

2 Phillip Darby, *The Fiction of Imperialism: Reading between International Relations and Postcolonialism* (London and Washington, DC: Cassell, 1998), 79. Subsequent references to this source will appear parenthetically within the text.

3 Suvendrini Perera's *Reaches of Empire: The English Novel from Edgeworth to Dickens* (New York: Columbia UP, 1991) focuses on novels written in the first half of the nineteenth century and before imperialism took firm hold of the British literary and cultural imagination. In these early works of fiction, Perera sees empire functioning "not as extraneous props or 'plot devices'" but instead "as productions of the defining oppositions between center and margins" (3). In *Imperialism at Home: Race and Victorian Women's Fiction* (Ithaca, NY: Cornell UP, 1996), Susan Meyer claims that though male writers such as Charles Dickens (1812–70) and Anthony Trollope (1815–82) frequently link white women with non-white colonized subjects in order to highlight an anxiety regarding British moral degeneracy, women authors use this link to call attention to general limitations of gender shared by both white British women and those colonized by the British (7). Like Meyer, Deirdre David in *Rule Britannia: Women, Empire, and Victorian Writing* (Ithaca, NY, and London: Cornell UP, 1995) sees connections between gender issues and colonialist critique, stating that "women, empire, and Victorian writing form a rich ideological cluster and a compelling subject for cultural analysis" (5).

nonexistent (i.e., Victorian women's intellectual involvement with issues of empire and colonized peoples) has been found to be fundamentally important to the understanding of women's imperial texts from the period. Although British women's moral influence over Indian women has been the subject of increased scholarly interest, relatively little has been said on the social position of biracial women in Anglo-India. One major exception is Indrani Sen's analysis of how Eurasian women, in particular, functioned in the British literary imagination and symbolized "deep-rooted colonial anxieties" (86). In addition to being a perceived threat to the imperial hierarchy due to the fact that, by blood, these women belonged to both cultural groups, Eurasians were repeatedly depicted as "intruders" who constantly strove to be on equal terms with the British ruling class (86–87). Because of this mixture of "black" and "white," these women were generally seen as inferior to both British and Indian women: "the factors of race, class and sexuality inflected the cultural constructions of Eurasian women with greater sensuality, weaker will power and, by inference, more proneness to 'immorality' than the 'native' woman" (48). With these "weaker" genetic qualities, Eurasian women were seen as a threat to the established cultural and racial superiority of the British because they had the ability to attract, marry, and eventually produce children with British men without initially revealing themselves as biracial: "European in her appearance as she is, the Eurasian woman, in a sense, signifies the black 'face' behind a near-white 'mask' and the marriage of the white man with the almost-white Eurasian woman is seen as a more immediate threat to Anglo-Indian imperial and ethnic identity" (88).[1] This attitude also points to deeper gender anxieties, as genetic deficiencies that derived from racial mixing were believed to originate in the Indian mother instead of the English father.

The Half-Caste: The Cultural Importance of Zillah Le Poer

Despite renewed interest in Dinah Mulock Craik, little has been written about her treatment of race and empire, particularly *The Half-Caste*, which appeared at a time when imperialism was beginning to take hold of India. The tale also appeared less than a decade before the Indian Uprising of 1857, an event that ulti-

1 For a discussion of how this anxiety regarding biracial women continued into twentieth-century Anglo-Indian fiction, see Glenn D'Cruz, *Midnight's Orphans: Anglo-Indians in Post/colonial Literature* (Bern and New York: Peter Lang, 2006), 33–35.

mately made Queen Victoria "Empress of India" and led to the formation of the infamous British Raj. *The Half-Caste* was first published in *Chambers's Papers for the People* (1851) and republished in two collections of Craik's fiction: *Avillion and Other Tales* (1853) and *Domestic Stories* (1859). A decade after her death in 1887, it was again republished as the lead tale in a collection titled *The Half-Caste* (1897).[1]

The story concerns the coming of age of its title character, the mixed-race Zillah Le Poer, daughter of an English merchant and an Indian princess. Sent back to England as a young girl, Zillah has no knowledge that she is an heiress who stands to inherit her mother's fortune. She lives with her uncle Le Poer, his wife, and two daughters and is treated as little more than a servant in the household. Zillah's situation is gradually improved when Cassandra Pryor is employed as a governess to the Le Poer daughters and takes an interest in the mysterious "cousin."

The Half-Caste remains relevant to today's readers for its examination of a biracial protagonist during Britain's increasing imperial involvement in India. Along with William Browne Hockley's "The Half-Caste Daughter" (1841), which is a less sympathetic exploration of the consequences of race mixing, it is one of the earliest works to focus on a female mixed-race character. Craik's novella defies contemporary stereotypes about the Eurasian population by portraying Zillah as an honest, beautiful, loyal, and sympathetic heroine. This portrayal is in direct contrast to widespread contemporary beliefs about the Eurasian community. As a result of increasing xenophobic tendencies and anxieties about such racial "mixing," which were seen as leading to the degeneration of the British population in India, these Eurasians, derogatively called "half-castes," were thought to inherit weakened genes that led to laziness, indecision, and stupidity.

Zillah Le Poer complicates all these misconceptions. With Zillah's eventual happy marriage to Andrew Sutherland, Craik anticipates by more than fifty years Maud Diver's (1867–1945) *Lilamani* (1911), which examines another successful English/Indian marriage. It is also important to note that while portrayals of successful mixed-race unions were extremely rare within the genre of Anglo-Indian popular fiction, marriages with equally happy offspring were even rarer. In *The Half-Caste*, Zillah and Andrew's marriage results in children, which was almost univer-

1 The following paragraphs discuss key elements of the plot in detail.

sally disapproved of, as such children were thought to be genetically weak. Kiran Mascarenhas has discussed how Zillah and Andrew's relationship is measured by eighteenth-century "class-based" rather than "race-based" standards. Mascarenhas goes on to say that Craik also refutes dualist views by portraying a character who is capable of improvement in a situation where two cultures merge through the biracial character.[1] Indeed, in her novella, Craik recalls the more lenient eighteenth-century notions of beneficial racial mixing and uses these beliefs in *The Half-Caste* in order to make an implicit comment that such ideas could help bring about greater trans-cultural understanding in the Great Britain of her day. In other words, race relations in 1850s England had much to learn from the cultural world of late eighteenth-century India.

In addition to issues of race and empire, Cassandra Pryor's initial feelings of "coming down in the world" after her family's loss of wealth, along with her feelings of loneliness and homesickness, are alleviated by her growing interest in the mysterious child whose past is deliberately kept from Cassandra by Zillah's outwardly respectable yet intensely controlling uncle. Zillah's uncle attempts to keep the child distant from British/white society by stressing the girl's perceived negative Indian qualities; he repeatedly refers to her as childish and ignorant. As Cassandra becomes increasingly determined to solve the mystery of Zillah's background, the once emotionally adrift governess finds a purpose in protecting the girl and secretly seeing to her improvement, against the wishes of the family.[2] *The Half-Caste* is thus not only about a biracial girl's moral and intellectual improvement as she turns from outcast victim to beloved heroine, but also about an English woman's ability to rise above her initial race prejudice, a cultural bias signified in the ways in which Cassandra frequently orientalizes Zillah early in the narrative. On first seeing Zillah, Cassandra says, "With some surprise I found her a half-caste girl—with an olive complexion, full Hindu lips, and eyes very black and bright. She was untidily dressed, which looked the

---

1 Kiran Mascarenhas, "*The Half-Caste*: A Half-Told Tale," *Women's Writing* 20.3 (2013): 350.

2 Sally Mitchell comments that the narrative has all the right elements for an effective mystery story, including "a gloomy Yorkshire estate, attempted elopements, intercepted letters, and dark secrets." Cassandra's incomplete understanding of the plot against Zillah also "adds a pleasurable irony" to the tale (*Dinah Mulock Craik* [Boston: Twayne, 1983], 25).

worse, since she was almost a woman; though her dull, heavy face had the stupidity of an ultra-stupid child" (p. 50). Reluctantly agreeing with Le Poer's description of Zillah as an "ugly little devil," she admits, "There was something quite demoniac in her black eyes at times. She was lazy, too—full of the languor of her native clime. Neither threats nor punishments could rouse her into the slightest activity" (p. 54). Yet Cassandra does not long share her employer's views, as she increasingly sympathizes with Zillah and secretly sets out to improve the girl's appearance, manners, and education. When Cassandra finds out that Zillah is actually the legitimate child of an English father and a wealthy Indian princess, she then takes it upon herself to save the girl before her fortune is stolen.

To add to the plot, Cassandra, a self-proclaimed "old maid" at age thirty, secretly loves Andrew Sutherland but remains a devoted friend even after her realization that he and Zillah are in love. These hints of a love triangle featuring a governess, along with its treatment of gender and race, make *The Half-Caste* an important counterpoint to Charlotte Brontë's *Jane Eyre* (1847). Both works depict the negative aspects of British imperial practices, but whereas Brontë depicts the "white Creole" Bertha Mason Rochester as a dangerous, unpredictable symbol of an empire that strikes back and has to be destroyed in order for the white heroine to have her happy ending, Craik's Zillah represents the potential for happiness in the imperial "other." This potential is developed by the care and support (both moral and pedagogical) of Cassandra. Instead of a mad wife and long-suffering governess that are set up as romantic rivals, Craik imagines a compassionate wife and maternal governess as the foundation of a lasting, supportive female relationship. This relationship is in many ways more daring than Brontë's vision of empire because it imagines what few people were willing or able to consider with regard to Anglo-Indian relations in the decade before the Indian Uprising. Craik's tale combines an examination of gender, race, and empire in a way that makes it a unique text among the numerous works of fiction published during Queen Victoria's reign. Both women, Zillah and Cassandra, are marginal characters who ultimately triumph over the stereotypical, limiting roles that society would otherwise choose for them.

Craik's characterization of Zillah Le Poer is a much more positive examination of mixed-race potential than her earlier treatment of the Scottish/Creole Christal Manners in *Olive* (1850). Christal is the daughter of Angus Rothesay and the West Indian

Creole Celia Manners. Celia and Christal follow Angus to England, where Celia works for a time as a painter's model. Though Olive notices Celia's beauty, she also sees that her face is "prematurely old" and tells "of a wrecked life."[1] Yet with her wasted beauty comes a fierceness that is often described in Western imaginings of the mysterious foreign "other." Celia holds her daughter "with a strain more like the gripe [*sic*] of a lioness than a tender woman's clasp" (130). She is then called a "poor creature" who "shriek[s] out Olive's surname, in tones so wild" that Olive cannot tell if it is "rage or entreaty" (132). Celia tells Olive her story, hinting at the in-between nature of her hybridity, which causes her to live half-slave and half-free. Likewise, Christal is described as having "fierce black eyes—the very image of a half-tamed gipsy" (131). After Celia's death, Christal is supported by Olive and her mother Sybilla Rothsay, who know nothing of Christal's connection to them as the product of Angus Rothsay's illicit affair. When Olive subsequently learns of her father's affair, she refers to Christal as her "poor sister" (287). Yet, as with her mother before her, Christal refuses to be shamed or pitied, responding, "*Sister!* And you are his child, his lawful child, while I—But you shall not live to taunt me. I will kill you, that you may go to your father, and mine, and tell him that I cursed him in his grave!" (287). She then attacks Olive in a "deadly embrace" and throws her to the floor. Before fleeing from the locked room, she looks at Olive "without pity or remorse" (287), further alluding to her "untamed" nature.

According to Cora Kaplan, Craik's novel "boldly borrows from and recasts the themes of empire and race in *Jane Eyre*, outing its racial subtext by giving literal embodiment to what is figuratively rendered in Brontë's novel."[2] Kaplan also argues that Craik takes issues of race further than does Brontë: "her views on race in *Olive* are at once more simply humanitarian and more explicitly grounded in biology than in *Jane Eyre*."[3] Though depicted in the same atavistic manner as Bertha Rochester, both Celia and Christal Manners are given a greater voice to express their

1 Dinah Mulock Craik, *Olive* (1850; Oxford and New York: Oxford UP, 1996), 130. Subsequent references will appear in parentheses within the text. For extracts from *Olive*, see Appendix B7.

2 Cora Kaplan, "Imagining Empire: History, Fantasy and Literature," *At Home with the Empire: Metropolitan Culture and the Imperial World*, ed. Catherine Hall and Sonya O. Rose (Cambridge: Cambridge UP, 2006), 207.

3 Kaplan 208.

suffering. Celia dies destitute, but she dies fiercely independent in her refusal to accept any financial help from Angus Rothesay. Christal is also more fully developed than Bertha, and though she is consigned to a convent by the novel's end, she finds some solace in teaching at the school, taking special interest in the orphans. However, Christal remains very much a "hybrid"—biologically, socially, and emotionally. She stays between the secular and religious worlds in the convent because she has not yet taken orders, thereby remaining "half-secular, half-nun-like" (327). And though she chooses to remain at the convent and seemingly finds some peace, Craik also describes the convent as "her spirit's grave" (329). Christal herself tells Olive that because of her suffering, she wants to remain dead to the outside world. This decision is two-sided. It is on her own terms—like her mother, she refuses to be "tyrannized over" by Olive or insulted by her half-sister's "hypocritical pity" (292). Yet any chance that Christal had for the more fulfilling and vibrant life that she dreamed of before learning the details of her birth are utterly closed to her because of her unresolved anger and mental suffering.

The colonial anxieties that dominate both *Olive* and *Jane Eyre* are neutralized in *The Half-Caste*. Though she shows signs of a temper, presumably inherited from her Indian mother, Zillah does not act on the anger that is so integral to the portrayal of Christal Manners or Bertha Rochester.[1] Putting this idea within a larger context, *The Half-Caste* serves as a reversal of the traditional colonial narrative of aggression and threatened violence. Reverse colonialization and fears of foreign invasion became popular fictional tropes for Victorian authors, as British fears for their safety increased amidst instability in their colonial territories in the latter half of the nineteenth century. In Craik's tale, this narrative is reversed as the colonial "other" is not the source of anxiety. Because of the machinations of her British uncle and cousin, Zillah is the one being pursued and in danger; her safety is being threatened. The fact that Zillah is non-threatening and ultimately likeable allows Craik another departure from contemporary colonial narratives. An integral part of the tale is the pro-

1 In addition to the heated temper associated with her perceived "uncivilized" Eastern temperament, Zillah's initially undeveloped mental faculties are blamed on her Indian mother as well, rather than on her lack of education and emotionally deprived upbringing. As Le Poer counsels Cassandra regarding his daughters and Zillah: "educate them all alike; at least so far as Zillah's small capacity allows.... her modicum of intellect is not greater than generally belongs to her mother's race" (p. 53).

gression of the Indian woman from oppressed *object* (how she can benefit a British man sexually or financially, or both) to beloved *person* (how she can be part of a mutually beneficial relationship through voluntarily sharing her wealth in a mutually happy marital union). By the end of the narrative, Zillah saves Andrew Sutherland in both romantic and commercial terms: her fortune saves him from financial ruin, thereby providing a home and continued comfort to both him and Cassandra. Yet, unlike the exploitative Indian labor practices that provided economic wealth and natural resources to Britain while leaving Indians themselves without economic advantage, Zillah shares her inheritance freely, ensuring her own well-being as well as that of her family and friends. Through both her wealth and her morality, Zillah assumes greater autonomy, thus giving her the secure place within British society frequently denied to other female symbols of empire.

Working Women and the Victorian Governess

There are many biographical similarities between Dinah Craik and Cassandra Pryor. After her father's refusal to continue his financial support of the family, followed seven months later by the death of her mother, Craik supported herself (and, for a time, her two brothers) as a writer. In 1845, she began her career by writing pieces for *Chambers's Edinburgh Journal*, and continued contributing poems, stories, and essays to the publication for the next ten years. Craik's subject matter and the mission of *Chambers's* were well-suited.[1] Discouraged by the cheap serials being published in London and Edinburgh in the 1830s, William Chambers (1800–83) sought to create a journal that would have a more substantive, educational content. In his memoir, Chambers recalls that current serials were "the perversion of what, if rightly conducted, might become a powerful engine of social improvement." He then "resolved to take advantage of the evidently growing taste for cheap literature, and lead it, as far as was in [his] power, in a

1 Craik's *The Half-Caste* was also part of a larger global emphasis maintained in the various essays and stories in *Chambers's Papers for the People* throughout its first decade. Along with Craik's tale in vol. 12, other works include the essays "The Incas of Peru," "European Intercourse with Japan," and "The Progress of America," as well as the story "Marfreda; Or, the Icelanders."

proper direction."[1] Shortly thereafter, in February 1832, Chambers and his brother Robert (1802–71) launched their journal, which quickly became a success. As a vehicle for forwarding educational reading content at an affordable price (originally three halfpence[2]), *Chambers's Edinburgh Journal* featured articles on literature, science, religion, and history.[3]

The need to provide for her own financial support enabled Craik to write from the point of view of an unmarried woman who had no one but herself on whom to depend. Shirley Foster has noted some seemingly disparate aspects of Craik's life and how "the dichotomies of Victorian female roles" affected her outlook as a writer. Because she remained single until she was 39, Craik gained a more complete understanding of a woman's unmarried life versus that of a married one.[4] Though she thought marriage a natural part of a woman's life, Craik also enjoyed her independence (though this independence was at first involuntary). Along with her friend, Frances Martin, Craik eventually established a comfortable residence in Camden Town.[5] In Margaret Shaen's *Memorials of Two Sisters* (1908), Craik and Martin are described as being "two handsome young girls, living in lodgings by themselves, writing books, and going about in society in the most independent manner, with their latch-key. Such a phe-

1 William Chambers, *Memoir of William and Robert Chambers* (Edinburgh and London: W & R. Chambers, 1884), 231.

2 The British halfpenny coin, which entered circulation in 1672, equaled half of a penny. "Three halfpence" was the common term used to describe 1½ pence. The halfpenny remained in circulation until July 1969, when British currency began transitioning to the decimal system, which took full effect in February 1971.

3 The success of the journal also led to other ventures, including *Chambers's Information for the People, Chambers's Educational Course, Miscellany of Useful and Entertaining Tracts, Chambers's Papers for the People*, and *Chambers's Encyclopedia*.

4 Shirley Foster, *Victorian Women's Fiction: Marriage, Freedom and the Individual* (London and Sydney: Croom Helm, 1985), 40.

5 Frances Martin (1829–1922) would later study philosophy and literature at the Ladies' College in London. In 1853, she became the first headmistress of the girls' school attached to the College. Martin's lifelong interest in women's education also led her to found the College for Working Women in 1874, renamed Frances Martin College in 1922. See her article, "A College for Working Women," *Macmillan's Magazine* (October 1879), 483–88.

nomenon was rare, perhaps unexampled in those days."[1] Craik's heroines in her fiction of the 1840s–1850s, written before her own marriage, are experiments in how a woman can achieve such autonomy, particularly her portrayal of governesses who ultimately choose work over marriage.

Cassandra Pryor is an important portrayal of the Victorian governess in literature, and she embodies many of the conflicting emotions that Craik herself felt. Cassandra is self-effacing yet independent, intelligent, and very much a role model for the Victorian moral life of support and self-sacrifice. She is devoted to her mother and makes the best out of her life when her financial situation declines and she must "seek a situation." As a narrator, though, Cassandra becomes an even more complex character, and it quickly becomes apparent to readers that her silences often speak more than her statements.[2] She is deeply protective of her charge, the neglected Zillah Le Poer, and comes to truly care about the girl's well-being. She takes on the responsibility of educating Zillah and rescuing her from the abuse she has suffered in the Le Poer household. Later on, Cassandra literally rescues Zillah from a disastrous elopement, and she remains stoical while Zillah, who has blossomed into an attractive and refined woman, marries the love of Cassandra's life. Yet, even though she, like other Craik characters, is "marked by the failure or deferment of the heterosexual marriage plot," this "failure" also gives Cassandra "some flexibility in gender roles."[3] She rejects an offer of marriage, travels to Italy, and then chooses to become a surrogate

---

1 Margaret Shaen, *Memorials of Two Sisters* (London: Longmans, Green, and Co., 1908), 64. Despite this independence, Craik also suffered from occasional loneliness, which added yet another dimension to her writing. Channeling her firsthand experience into fiction, Showalter says, Craik "specialized in tales of women's suffering and endurance" (7), and it is this focus that endeared her to the British female reading public, if not always to her critics. See especially, "The Lady Novelists of Great Britain" (*Gentlemen's Magazine* 40, July 1853), R.H. Hutton's "Novels by the Authoress of 'John Halifax,'" (*North British Review* 29, 1858), and "The Author of *John Halifax*" (*British Quarterly Review* 44, July 1866).

2 Kiran Mascarenhas argues that a reading of Cassandra Pryor as narrator of *The Half-Caste* enlightens examination (or reexamination) of Phineas Fletcher's function as narrator of *John Halifax*, saying, "Phineas is so successfully repressed, and John so very heroic, that the reader's attention is more firmly directed away from the narrator in *John Halifax* than in *The Half-Caste*. Revisiting *John Halifax* after reading *The Half-Caste*, however, one cannot help but pay more attention to Phineas" (353).

3 Mascarenhas 351.

aunt to Zillah and Andrew Sutherland's daughter, also named Cassandra. She becomes a writer as well, who, unfulfilled and repressed as she may be, has the freedom to tell her own story.

In addition to her portrayal of Cassandra Pryor, Craik detailed the trials of the unmarried governess in *Bread upon the Waters: A Governess's Life* (1852), which Shirley Foster calls "Craik's most interesting portrayal of permanent spinsterhood."[1] After her father remarries, Felicia Lyne and her two younger brothers fall victim to their stepmother, who manipulates her husband into distancing himself from his children. Having no choice but to leave her childhood home when she comes of age, Felicia decides to become a governess. She initially finds teaching difficult but needs the money in order to survive. Using Felicia Lyne as her mouthpiece, Craik incorporates frequent social commentary about the impoverished position of governesses in early Victorian Britain. Looking back on her earlier years and remembering how degraded she felt, Felicia recalls how she took her first position for granted: "It must have been some charitable soul who gave me through pity what I took as an ordinary right, not knowing how many a poor unknown, uncredentialed governess waits, hopes, doubts, gradually sinks down lower and lower, despairs, and starves."[2] She frequently comments on her changed situation, saying that if any of her former friends saw her, they would not recognize her because of her careworn appearance and shabby clothes. After years of denying herself any happiness—for a governess, "pleasure must always yield to duty" (*Bread* 145)—Felicia reconnects with a former acquaintance, Sir Godfrey Redwood. Much like Cassandra and Andrew Sutherland, Felicia

---

1 Foster 59. Craik published the tale for the Governesses' Benevolent Institution. Established in 1843, it had two arms: the Governesses' Annuity Fund (money raised by subscription for women in need of extra funds) and the Governesses' Provident Fund (intended to help women invest their money). Throughout its existence, the Institution was severely underfunded. In its first year, only a little over half those applying for financial aid were funded. The Institution had raised nearly £180,000 by 1859, but there were still too many applicants for everyone in need to receive money. For more on the Institution, see Ruth Brandon, *Governess: The Lives and Times of the Real Jane Eyres* (New York: Walker & Company, 2008), 226–28.

2 Dinah Craik, *Bread upon the Waters: A Governess's Life* (London: Governesses' Benevolent Institution, 1852), 130. Subsequent parenthetical references are to this edition. For extracts from *Bread upon the Waters*, see Appendix C5.

harbors a long-standing secret love for Sir Godfrey, an emotion that she tries to deny to herself (and, as narrator, to the reader as well). With his help, she becomes the governess to a wealthy earl's daughter. At 31 years old, Felicia tells the reader she is happy with her life, but like Cassandra, her frequent self-denials call into question if this is indeed the whole truth. She consequently becomes a very unreliable narrator, full of half-truths and unspoken longing. Her refusal to admit any regret brings that very sense of regret to light.

Felicia Lyne's inability to regain her youthful hopes and dreams is expressed when, playing on a tree swing with her younger charges, Felicia suddenly crashes into a tree and becomes permanently crippled. As with other Craik narratives, Felicia's unspoken frustration is outwardly expressed through her lameness. Regarding Craik's disabled heroines, Elaine Showalter has discussed how she sought to show the extent to which unmarried women were figurative cripples, women who were "thwarted in the only role which endowed their lives with meaning and weight; freaks in a society that had no use for them."[1]

By the story's end, Felicia is almost 50 years old, crippled, and living with her brother's family in her "Bird's Nest" (168). Like Cassandra, Felicia is trying to finish her journal, and as she thinks about her life, she hears her nieces and nephews running around her. Though she says that she is "as busy as busy can be" (167), she is confined to her room most of the time because of her nearly complete inability to walk. Felicia also insists that she is happy, despite having "occasional fits of depression, hard enough to bear" (168). As the last words of the narrative make plain, her thoughts are still centered on Sir Godfrey and, as with the case of Cassandra Pryor and her continued devotion to Andrew Sutherland, bittersweet remembrances of what could have been.

The plight of the Victorian governess had been made popular a few years before Craik's two governess tales, in Charlotte Brontë's *Jane Eyre* and Anne Brontë's *Agnes Grey*, both published in 1847.[2] Readers can see the influence of *Jane Eyre* in both of

1 Showalter 11.

2 Anne Brontë (1820–49), youngest child of the Brontë family, worked as a governess for two Yorkshire families from 1839 to 1845. Her first position with the Ingham family at Blake Hall, Mirfield, lasted less than a year. In 1840, Anne took another position with the Robinson family at Thorp Green Hall, Little Ouseburn. Her unhappiness during this time and the difficulties she experienced served as the inspiration for *Agnes Grey*. Her second and final novel was *The Tenant of Wildfell Hall* (1848).

Craik's works, as well as her experimentation with the standard formula of the governess narrative: the heroine of the story is a single woman who falls on hard times; she is suddenly impoverished, left without family support, and must make her own way in the world. These novels then describe the drudgery and loneliness of governess life, as these women were often liminal figures, occupying a social no man's land: not "low" enough to be part of the servant class, but not "ladylike" enough to be part of the family employing her. In some cases, the governess is rewarded for her perseverance by winning the love and devotion of her (often initially mysterious and aloof) male employer. What is interesting in both of Craik's governess works is that the women are rewarded with financial security and a degree of independence, but this is not accomplished through marriage. Because of a need to remain autonomous (and because of disappointed love that remains largely unexpressed), both Felicia Lyne and Cassandra Pryor choose to remain single and must experience the more traditional life of marriage and children vicariously through the surrogate families with which they live. Yet as narrators, both women also refuse to outwardly acknowledge their respective failed romances, presumably as a coping mechanism. Because of this lingering sense of an unfulfilled life lived "apart," Craik's happy endings for both Cassandra and Felicia are open to interpretation.

Debates about the status of governesses predominated in Craik's time. "Hints on the Modern Governess System," which appeared in the November 1844 issue of *Fraser's Magazine*, deplores the current social structure that allows governesses to live in abject poverty with little hope of any future improvement. According to the author, the problem started when the growing surplus of single women meant that they had to learn to support themselves and therefore could not depend on the traditional prospect of marriage. Many of these women chose governessing as a means of earning money. However, this, in turn, created a surplus of teachers, and the inevitable law of supply and demand worked against these desperate women.[1] As a remedy to some of the problems encountered by the governess, the author advocates increased education—the better qualified, the better their reputations will become. Women are also encouraged to leave the profession in order to increase demand. Other career options that

1 "Hints on the Modern Governess System," *Fraser's Magazine* 30 (November 1844): 572, 573. See Appendix C1.

suit the abilities of the governess include clerks and bookkeepers.[1] While clerking was a possibility, according to the author, trade was strictly forbidden. Sarah Stickney Ellis (1799–1872), in *The Women of England* (1839), summed up this cultural employment barrier by saying that while men could choose practically any profession in order to support a household, "if a lady does but touch any article, no matter how delicate, in the way of trade, she loses caste, and ceases to be a lady."[2] Sarah Lewis's "On the Social Position of Governesses" (see Appendix C2), published in the April 1848 issue of *Fraser's Magazine*, also condemns the current efforts to improve the situation of these women. Lewis, having worked as a governess, highlights the conflicting ideals of her society, as people increasingly believe in the importance of education but refuse to allow that those who do a good part of that teaching are equally important members of the educational community. To rectify this, Lewis suggests that the government take greater responsibility in regulating the governess system through written public examinations in order to establish standards within the profession. This, in turn, would ensure that only competent women are allowed to practice, thereby raising the reputation of the whole group.[3]

The letters of Charlotte Brontë provide another example of the difficulties experienced by the Victorian governess. From May to July 1839, Brontë took a temporary position as governess

---

1 "Hints" 580.

2 Sarah Ellis, *The Women of England: Their Social Duties and Domestic Habits* (1839; London, Fisher, Son, and Co., 1845), 463. The term "caste" is also frequently used in contemporary writings to describe a governess's lessened social status. This idea of a precarious social standing provides a further connection between Cassandra Pryor and Zillah Le Poer in *The Half-Caste*. The topic of women's equality and their right to seek employment was taken up in several publications, including Barbara Leigh Smith's (1827–91) *Women and Work* (1857), Harriet Martineau's (1802–76) "Female Industry" (published in the *Edinburgh Review* in 1859), John Duguid Milne's (1822–89) *Industrial and Social Position of Women in the Middle and Lower Ranks* (1857), and Bessie Rayner Parkes's (1829–1925) *Essays on Women's Work* (1865), which was largely reprinted from the *English Woman's Journal*. Each argues for meaningful employment that gave women purpose, independence, and allowed them to feel useful.

3 Sarah Lewis, "On the Social Position of Governesses," *Fraser's Magazine* (April 1848): 413. Craik also echoed this view in Chapter 3 ("Female Professions") of *A Woman's Thoughts about Women* (1858); see Appendix A1.

to the Sidgwick family near Skipton, North Yorkshire. Her correspondence from the time describes her dissatisfaction during her time there. She quickly comes to the conclusion that "a private governess has no existence, is not considered as a living and rational being except as connected with the wearisome duties she has to fulfil. While she is teaching the children, working for them, amusing them, it is all right. If she steals a moment for herself she is a nuisance."[1] These difficulties point to the undefined position shared by Brontë and her fellow governesses. According to Kathryn Hughes, the Victorian upper-middle-class family was at this time increasingly defining itself according to a hierarchical social structure. This meant that such families saw themselves "as a microcosm of society at large, a self-sufficient kingdom, complete with ruler, consort, subjects and lower orders."[2] Yet, within this system, there was no "middle-class" reserved for the governess.[3] The financial and social insecurities of governesses gradually lessened as the century progressed and women were granted greater opportunities for employment outside the house.

Zillah's Sisters: Nineteenth-Century Depictions of Eurasian Women

Eurasian characters appear in many works of nineteenth-century fiction, but these portrayals are typically limited to undeveloped supporting roles and unflattering stereotypes. An exception is Ezra Jennings, a character in Wilkie Collins's *The Moonstone* (1868). Though not as fully developed as the other major characters in the novel, Jennings possesses a more complex background than previous depictions of biracial characters and is integral in helping to solve the mystery at the center of Collins's novel. Heroic Indian women have fared somewhat better in nineteenth-century fiction, a prominent example being Philip Meadows Taylor's *Seeta* (1872).[4] Beautiful and intelligent, Seeta

1 Charlotte Brontë, *The Letters of Charlotte Brontë*, vol. 1, ed. Margaret Smith (Oxford: Clarendon, 1995), 191. For relevant extracts from Brontë's letters, see Appendix C4.

2 Kathryn Hughes, *The Victorian Governess* (London and Rio Grande, OH: Hambledon P, 1993), 86.

3 Hughes 86.

4 Philip Meadows Taylor's (1808–76) novels tend to be more sympathetic toward Indo-British relations than those of his contemporaries. This idea of interracial acceptance and harmony between Indian and British culture was mirrored in Taylor's own life. He married Mary (*continued*)

sacrifices herself to save her English husband during the Indian Uprising of 1857. Still rarer, however, are depictions of female Eurasian main characters, who, like Zillah Le Poer, are given detailed personalities that make them more than mere set pieces.

One of the earliest attempts to portray a female Eurasian main character is Anne Berners in William Browne Hockley's "The Half-Caste Daughter" (1841). Although largely ambivalent about race and empire, Hockley examines the social dynamics of the Anglo-Indian community and its resistance to allowing mixed-race members to enter British society in India. After being sent to England as a girl in order to be educated, Anne returns to her father's home in India. Colonel Berners feels tremendous guilt over his past "crime,"[1] a relationship with an Indian woman which resulted in the birth of his daughter. Although he knows that Anne is both beautiful and educated, Berners realizes that his daughter will have a difficult time being accepted by his fellow British. He enlists the help of Mrs. Alton, the second most influential woman in Madras. Mrs. Alton hesitates to chaperone Anne because of her own prejudice, but finally agrees out of a selfish motivation to best a rival whose daughter is the current belle of the colonial community. On her way to the colonel's home, "to see what kind of an animal the girl was" (192), Mrs. Alton fears that Anne will be too dark to "pass" within Anglo-Indian society.[2]

Palmer, the Eurasian granddaughter of William Palmer (1740–1816), and his efforts at improvement and reform won him the appreciation and loyalty of the Indians with whom he lived and worked as a magistrate. For extracts from *Seeta*, see Appendix B6.

1 William Browne Hockley, "The Half-Caste Daughter," *The Widow of Calcutta; The Half-Caste Daughter; and Other Sketches*, vol. 2 (London: D.N. Carvalho, 1841), 184. Subsequent parenthetical references are to this edition. For the complete story, see Appendix B5.

2 Skin color was vital in determining a Eurasian woman's chances of establishing herself in Anglo-Indian society. John Mawson's description of "The Eurasian Belle," published as part of his *A Few Local Sketches* (Calcutta, 1844), claimed, "Truly, setting aside *the tint*, which after all is hardly skin-deep, your Eurasian belle is a very comely girl. Her portrait *in colours* might not win much admiration from the critical and fastidious Briton; but in a *plain* steel engraving, would not those neatly moulded and highly polished features, and above all, those large lustrous black eyes, with their long silky fringes, render it well worth a place in the Book of Beauty[?]" This "Eurasian belle" equals the beauty "of the fairest and noblest of England's daughters.... Yet [her] bust or the portrait would be but the likeness of an humble East Indian girl, sneered at under the denomination of a *half-caste*, a *chee-chee*, or 'one of the

Yet her fears are allayed once she sees Anne's remarkable beauty. During this first encounter, Mrs. Alton is able to admire Anne's beauty and natural grace, but she is unable to see her as anything more than a pawn in her game to gain the social advantage over her rivals, Mrs. Browne and her daughter Kitty.

Throughout the story, the narrator comments on the difficulties facing Anne as she attempts to gain social acceptance in Madras. Both "the intelligent" and "the good" see her as part "of a race born of shame,—whose inheritance was the vices of both parents, the virtues of neither. Willing to admit the abstract truth, that the human mind is formed by education and habit, they denied the application of it to particulars" (196–97). This subtle didacticism is followed by further comments that if a British man were to marry a mixed-race woman, he would inevitably regret it.[1] Yet Hockley prefers to remain in the abstract when thinking of Anne as an individual. The reader never knows her well. Instead of being allowed to realize her full potential, Anne, under the tutelage of Mrs. Alton, chooses to marry strategically in order to secure her place within Anglo-Indian society. Her marriage to Sir Henry Tresham, a chief justice, is Anne's "one avenue of escape" (201). His high standing in the community will consequently serve to erase her "stain" (192) of Indian blood. Even though Hockley does not give his readers a detailed sense of Anne as a person, he is clear on what the prejudice of Anglo-Indian society

---

Browns'" (87, 88; italics in original). In *The Half-Caste*, Craik seems less concerned with the social ramifications of skin color, though Cassandra continues to identify Zillah's beauty as "Eastern" throughout the narrative and remarks that Zillah looks "like a princess out of the *Arabian Nights*." Cassandra also comments on how Zillah's color affects her beauty, while at the same time she reverts to the derogatory term of "half-caste" in order to describe her friend: "Even though her skin was that of a half-caste, and her little hands were not white but brown, there was no denying that she was a very beautiful woman" (p. 83).

1 Despite Hockley's comments about the general societal prejudice against such marriages, there were exceptions. For instance, Thomas Skinner's *Excursions in India* (1832) notes that "Half-caste women are frequently chosen by the British soldiers for their wives, and I believe they make extremely good ones. In habits and morals, I am sorry to say, they are far before our own countrywomen of the same class in the East, and the domestic comforts of the two families are not to be compared" (1: 215–16). Testifying before a parliamentary committee in 1853, the Indian civil servant (and later governor of Madras) Charles Trevelyan (1807–86) expressed much the same sentiment, declaring that Eurasian women made excellent wives and mothers (see Ballhatchet, 99–100).

ultimately does to her. She is turned into a heartless opportunist who must deceive others in order to avoid ostracism. She likewise must deny herself the possibility of love in order to secure her place in society and to protect herself from future prejudice. Anne stoically sums up her fate, saying, "I might have been a happier woman, but that is a rôle quite out of the sphere of an intellectual *half-caste*" (204). In using the derogatory term, Anne is admitting a full understanding of how she is viewed by her fellow British. She must become something unnatural, always overcompensating for her racial background and the "sins" of her parents.

This pull of a troubled past is much less evident in *The Half-Caste*. Zillah's parents remain in the background of the story, and her dominant connections with them—in particular, her mother—are only those things that ultimately benefit Zillah: her beauty and her wealth. Any cultural "sin" in the narrative is transfigured into crimes committed against her Indian mother and Zillah herself. Early in the story, Zillah accuses her English father, whom she remembers as an "ugly, horrible-looking man," of stealing her mother's diamond ring (pp. 56–57). Later, Cassandra learns more about how the Le Poer family plans to control the inheritance that belongs more to Zillah's aristocratic Indian mother than to her English father. Matilda Le Poer reveals the extent of the family plot, telling the governess, "Zillah will then be very rich, as her father left her all he had; and uncle Henry was a great nabob, because he married an Indian princess, and got all her money. Now you see ... we must be very civil to Zillah, and of course she will give us all her money" (p. 70). Unlike Anne Berners, who inherits beauty but also cultural shame from an Indian mother in "The Half-Caste Daughter," Zillah's mother is depicted as a beautiful Indian princess, a woman who possesses more beauty, wealth, and morality than her English relations.

After the cultural trauma of the Indian Uprising in 1857, positive portrayals of biracial characters became even more uncommon. A rare instance of a Eurasian heroine can be found in Fanny Emily Penny's *Caste and Creed* (1890), an Anglo-Indian romance novel in which Zelma Anderson, the daughter of a Scottish merchant and his Brahmin wife, exhibits the best qualities of both races.[1] She ben-

1 Fanny Emily (Farr) Penny (1847–1939), also known as "F.E. Penny" and "Mrs. Frank Penny," spent many years in India as the wife of a British missionary. She steadily published Anglo-Indian romances up until her death. Many of her novels deal with issues of racial identity and cultural intermingling, for example, *A Mixed Marriage* (1903) and *A Question of Colour* (1926).

efits from her years of schooling in England and returns to India a seemingly perfect balance of sense and sensibility. Zelma is devoted to her father but grows increasingly disheartened by what she sees as her mother's less-disciplined habits and religious superstitions. Zelma's character and manners ensure that she is wholeheartedly accepted by the Anglo-Indian community, and by the novel's end she achieves a successful, mutually loving marriage with the Englishman Percy Bell. Intellectual and disciplined, Percy is the only man thought by the other characters to be a worthy match for Zelma. In the last sentence of the novel, he sums up the unique balance of East and West that exists within Zelma: she is both a "rose" and a "lotus," and ultimately his "perfect wife."[1]

A far less flattering (yet still sympathetic) depiction of a Eurasian protagonist is the title character in Mary Churchill Luck's *Poor Elisabeth* (1901).[2] Well liked and popular while at school in England, Elisabeth Murray makes friends easily, and on her arrival in India, much like Anne Berners in "The Half-Caste Daughter," she has no idea that her mixed-race background has already cast a social stigma on her identity. Her seemingly infinite kindness and emotional potential are constantly being checked by the ultra-rational and prejudiced English colonials that make up her family and community and who alternately feel either pity or hatred toward her. Elisabeth's doom is a direct comment on the wider Anglo-Indian society's failure to make room for such people who do not conform to their strict moral standards. Early in the narrative, Elisabeth speaks with more meaning than she knows and sums up both her own personal tragedy and the greater tragedy of those like her: "it seems a pity because one race is dark and another fair that they can never be friends. And I thought perhaps someone who had some of the blood of each, even though not a clever person, could understand better."[3] Though Mary Churchill Luck is able to have her main character give voice to this cultural tragedy, it is a tragedy that remained largely ignored by British society well into the twentieth century.

---

1 Fanny Emily Penny, *Caste and Creed*, 2 vols. (London: F. V. White, 1890), 2:220.

2 Mary Churchill Luck (1869–1949) wrote under the pseudonym "M. Hamilton." After her marriage to Churchill Arthur Luck in Lahore, Bengal, in 1898, she spent the next 20 years living in India before settling in England. The majority of her novels are set in her native Ireland.

3 M. Hamilton [Mary Churchill Luck], *Poor Elisabeth* (London: Hurst and Blackett, 1901), 14.

American writer Helen Blackmar Maxwell's *The Way of Fire* (1897) has a sympathetic and likeable biracial heroine at the center of the tale.[1] The novel, whose main character is similar to Penny's portrayal of Zelma in *Caste and Creed*, tends toward didacticism in parts. It tells the story of Annie Swinton, who sums up her Eurasian status by stating, "I have never been able to claim a nationality, and might properly be called 'A Woman without a Country.'"[2] Yet, through her winning personality, Annie manages to win over not only the upper-classes of Anglo-Indian society in both India and England, but also her own husband, who, having originally regretted marrying a biracial woman, learns to both love and appreciate her. Through a series of mutual misunderstandings and miscommunications, Maxwell makes it apparent that the once-snobbish and socially ambitious Dr. Payne Swinton must improve himself and overcome his own shortcomings, much more than Annie has to overcome hers. Their strengthened union also ultimately strengthens the Anglo-Indian society of Kaiserpur, where ancestry becomes less important than individual merit. The town becomes more tolerant of Eurasians, largely because of the positive influence of Annie, "whose sweetness and charm are universally conceded."[3] Annie's balance of beauty, kindness, and intelligence, much like that possessed by Zelma in Penny's *Caste and Creed*, can be read as the continuing realization of a more fully developed portrayal of a biracial character, a type that began with Zillah Le Poer in *The Half-Caste*. As Cassandra says near the end of the narrative, Zillah was a woman who "had grown up beautiful in mind as well as in body" (p. 78).

Considering Dinah Mulock Craik's involvement with issues of gender, race, and empire gives readers a new dimension in discussing the cultural value of her writing. For many years she was

---

1 Helen Blackmar (Maxwell) Barker (1852–1938) was born in West Springfield, Pennsylvania. She was the daughter of Protestant missionaries who moved their family to India when Helen was a girl. She married the Rev. Allen J. Maxwell (1851–90) in 1879 and, after his death in Lucknow in 1890, turned to writing in order to support herself and her daughter, Louise. She and Louise moved to Hawaii, where Helen married Albert S. Barker (1845–1916), a United States naval officer, in 1894. Her novels include *The Bishop's Conversion* (1892), *Three Old Maids in Hawaii* (1896), and *The Way of Fire* (1897). Her name is also given as Ellen Blackmar Maxwell.

2 Helen Blackmar Maxwell, *The Way of Fire* (New York: Dodd, Mead and Company, 1897), 60.

3 Maxwell 243.

recognized as a sentimental writer, a children's author, and an insular champion of conservative Victorian values; however, through works such as *The Half-Caste*, Craik emerges as a part of a much larger literary debate about British racial attitudes both in and out of England. By having the empire come into the English domestic home and ultimately thrive there, Craik marks an important instance of how India and its people could function within British society. Written in 1851, at a time when racial boundaries were becoming both more defined and increasingly restrictive, *The Half-Caste* breaks with contemporary prejudice against the foreign "other" and offers an imaginative possibility about the benefits of cultural mixing, a union represented in a female biracial character who goes from being a victim of empire to become a well-respected British wife, mother, and loyal friend. After the Indian Uprising of 1857, it would take many years before such characters could be imagined again.

Dinah Mulock Craik: A Brief Chronology

1826	Dinah Maria Mulock born on 20 April in Stoke-on-Trent, eldest child of Thomas Mulock and Dinah Mellard Mulock.
1827	Tom Mulock (brother) born.
1829	Benjamin Mulock (brother) born.
1831	Family moves to Newcastle-under-Lyme.
1839	Family moves to London.
1841	Publishes verses (under "D.M.M.") in the *Staffordshire Advertiser*.
1844	Accompanied by her mother and brothers, separates from the emotionally unstable Thomas Mulock.
1845	"Good Seed" (poem) published in *Chambers's Edinburgh Journal* in July. Her mother dies on 3 October. Assumes the domestic and financial responsibilities of supporting her two brothers.
1846	Continues to publish poems and stories in *Chambers's*. *Michael the Miner* (children's book) published by the Religious Tract Society.
1847	Publishes stories in *Dublin University Magazine* and continues to publish in *Chambers's*. Her brother Tom (a merchant ship crew member) dies in February after suffering injuries from a fall from a ship.
1848	Publishes in *Dublin University Magazine*, *Sharpe's London Magazine*, *Fraser's Magazine*, and *Douglas Jerrold's Shilling Magazine*. *How to Win Love; or Rhoda's Lesson* (children's book) published.
1849	*Cola Monti; or the Story of a Genius* (children's book) and first novel, *The Ogilvies* (3 vols.), published.
1850	*Olive* (3 vols.) published. Her brother Ben moves to Australia. After his departure, shares lodgings with friend, Frances Martin.
1851	*The Half-Caste: An Old Governess's Tale* published in vol. 12 of *Chambers's Papers for the People*.
1852	*Bread upon the Waters; A Governess's Life* published to benefit the Governesses' Benevolent Institution. *The Head of the Family* (3 vols.) and *Alice Learmont: A Fairy Tale* (children's book) published.

1853	*Agatha's Husband* (3 vols.) and *A Hero: Philip's Book* (children's book) published. First collection of short fiction published as *Avillion and Other Tales* (3 vols., with *The Half-Caste* in vol. 3).
1855	*The Little Lychetts* (children's book) published, as well as stories in *Fraser's Magazine* and *Household Words*, and essays in *Chambers's Edinburgh Journal.*
1856	*John Halifax, Gentleman* (3 vols.), a best-seller, published.
1857	*A Woman's Thoughts about Women* published as a series of essays in *Chambers's Edinburgh Journal. Nothing New* (short stories) published.
1858	*A Woman's Thoughts about Women* published.
1859	*A Life for a Life* (3 vols.) published. Two more collections of short stories, *Romantic Tales* and *Domestic Stories* (including *The Half-Caste*), published. *Poems* published. On her increased earnings, moves to Wildwood cottage (Hampstead) and entertains other writers.
1860	*Our Year: A Children's Book in Prose and Verse* published. Begins writing articles for *Macmillan's Magazine.*
1861	*Studies from Life* (collected essays) published. Writes "To Novelists—and a Novelist" for April 1861 issue of *Macmillan's* (containing a review of George Eliot's *The Mill on the Floss*).
1862	*Mistress and Maid* published in *Good Words.* Assumes the care of her brother Ben, then returned from Australia and increasingly unstable.
1863	*The Fairy Book* (children's book) published. Writes articles for *Macmillan's* and *Cornhill. Mistress and Maid* (2 vols.) published. Ben is injured after escaping from a lunatic asylum and dies in June.
1864	Receives an honorary Civil List Pension of £60 per year.
1865	*Christian's Mistake* published. Also publishes *A New Year's Gift to Sick Children* (poems) for the benefit of the Edinburgh Children's Hospital. Marries Scottish writer and historian George Lillie Craik (1839–1905) on 29 April in Bath.
1866	*A Noble Life* (2 vols.) published.
1867	Writes travel articles for *Good Words. Two Marriages* (2 vols.) published.
1868	*The Woman's Kingdom* published in *Good Words.*

1869 Adopts abandoned baby (named Dorothy) in January. *A Brave Lady* published in *Macmillan's* (1869–70). *The Woman's Kingdom* (3 vols.) published. The Craiks move into new home, "Corner House" (near Bromley). Her father dies in August.

1870 *The Unkind Word and Other Stories* (2 vols.) and *A Brave Lady* (3 vols.) published.

1871 *Hannah* published in *Saint Paul's*. Also publishes *Fair France: Impressions of a Traveller* and *Little Sunshine's Holiday: A Picture from Life* (children's book). Edits *Twenty Years Ago: From the Journal of a Girl in Her Teens*.

1872 *The Adventures of a Brownie, as Told to My Child* (for Dorothy) and *Hannah* (2 vols.) published. Collects and edits *Is It True? Tales Curious and Wonderful*.

1874 *My Mother and I: A Girl's Love-Story* published in *Good Words* and later by Isbister.

1875 *The Little Lame Prince and His Travelling Cloak* (children's book), *Sermons Out of Church* (essays), and *Songs of Our Youth* (poems) published.

1876 *The Laurel Bush: An Old-Fashioned Love Story* published in *Good Words*.

1877 *The Laurel Bush* published.

1878 Edits *A Legacy: Being the Life and Remains of John Martin, Schoolmaster and Poet* (2 vols.).

1879 *Young Mrs. Jardine* published in *Good Words* and later in three volumes.

1880 *Thirty Years: Poems Old and New* published.

1881 *His Little Mother and Other Tales and Sketches* published.

1882 *Plain Speaking* (essays) published.

1884 *Miss Tommy: A Medieval Romance* published. "An Unsentimental Journey through Cornwall" published in *English Illustrated Magazine* and later by Macmillan.

1886 *King Arthur: Not a Love Story* and *About Money and Other Things* (essays and children's stories) published. Writes essays for *English Illustrated Magazine*, *Contemporary Review*, and *Nineteenth Century*.

1887 *Fifty Golden Years* (for Queen Victoria's Jubilee) published. *An Unknown Country* (travel narrative about Northern Ireland) published in *English Illustrated Magazine* and later by Macmillan. Writes essays for *Cornhill*, *Contemporary Review*, and *Good Words*. Dies of heart failure on 12 October.

A Note on the Text

The present text is based on the 1897 edition of *The Half-Caste* published as the lead tale in *The Half-Caste: An Old Governess's Tale* by W. & R. Chambers (London and Edinburgh). An identical version was also published in 1897 by Thomas Whittaker (New York). These texts correct punctuation and tense issues found in earlier editions. Significant differences between the 1897 Chambers and New York editions, the original 1851 edition published in *Chambers's Papers for the People* (vol. 12, no. 94), and the 1853 and 1859 texts are noted in this Broadview Edition.

The Half-Caste
An Old Governess's Tale[1]

BY THE AUTHOR OF

'JOHN HALIFAX, GENTLEMAN'

WITH PREFATORY LETTER BY THE AUTHOR

W. & R. CHAMBERS, LIMITED
LONDON AND EDINBURGH
1897

1 The 1851 text has "Tale," while the 1897 text has "Tale" on the title page (reproduced here) but switches to "Story" in the Contents and at the beginning of the narrative. The 1897 text also drops the original subtitle, "Founded on Fact."

"We know what we are, but we know not what we may be," as my quaintly-clever niece and name-child, Cassia, would say.[1] And, truly, who could have thought that I, a plain governess, should in my old age have become a writer? Yet, for the life of me, I cannot invent a plot—I must write nothing but truth. Here I pause, recollecting painfully that in my first sentence I have sinned against truth by entitling Cassia "my niece and name-child," when, strictly speaking, she is neither the one nor the other. She is no blood-relation at all, and my own name happens to be Cassandra. I always disliked it heartily until Mr. Sutherland called me—But I forget that I must explain a little. Mr. Sutherland was—no, thank Heaven!—*is*, a very good man; a friend of my late father, and of the same business—an Indian merchant. When, in my twenty-fifth year, my dear father died, and we were ruined—a quiet way of expressing this, but in time one learns to speak so quietly of every pang—Mr. Sutherland was very kind to my mother and to me. I remember, as though it were yesterday, one day when he sat with us in our little parlour, and hearing my mother calling me "Cassie," said laughingly that I always put him in mind of a certain Indian spice. "In fact," he added, looking affectionately at my dear, gentle little mother, and approvingly—yes, it was approvingly, at me—"in fact, I think we three sitting thus, with myself in the centre, might be likened to myrrh, aloes, and cassia."[2] One similitude was untrue; for he was not bitter, but "sweet as summer."[3] However, from that time he always

---

1 The 1853 and 1859 texts have "'We know what we are, but we know not what we may be,' as my quaintly clever niece and name-child, Cassia, a great reader and quoter of Shakspeare, would say." Ophelia's lines spoken to the King and Queen in William Shakespeare's (1564–1616) *Hamlet*: "They say the owl was a baker's daughter. Lord, we know what we are but know not what we may be" (4.5.42–44). The lines are inspired by an English folktale about a baker's daughter who refused to give the disguised Jesus some bread and so was turned into an owl.

2 "All thy garments smell of myrrh, and aloes, and cassia" (Psalm 45:8).

3 Griffith's description of Cardinal Wolsey, spoken to Queen Katherine in Shakespeare's *King Henry VIII*:

> This cardinal,
> Though from a humble stock, undoubtedly
> Was fashioned to much honour from his cradle.
> He was a scholar, and a ripe and good one;
> Exceeding wise, fair-spoken, and persuading;
> Lofty and sour to them that loved him not,
> But, to those men that sought him, sweet as summer. (4.2.48–54)

called me Cassia. I rather like the name; and latterly it was very kind of him to—— There, I am forestalling my history again!

When I was twenty-five, as I said, I first went out as a governess. This plan was the result of many consultations between my mother and myself. A hard thing was my leaving home; but I found I could thereby earn a larger and more regular salary, part of which, being put by, would some time enable me to live altogether with my mother. Such were her plannings and hopes for the future. As for my own—— But it is idle to dwell upon things so long past. God knew best, and it all comes to the same at the end of life. It was through Mr. Sutherland that I got my first situation. He wrote my mother a hurried letter, saying he had arranged for me to enter a family, concerning whom he would explain before my departure. But something hindered his coming; it was a public meeting, I remember, for though still a young man, he was held in much honour among the City merchants, and knew the affairs of India well from early residence there. Of course, having these duties to fulfil, it was natural he should not recollect my departure; so I started without seeing him, and without knowing more of my future abode than its name, and that of my employer. It was a Yorkshire village, and the gentleman whose family I was going to was a Mr. Le Poer. My long journey was dreary—God knows how dreary! In youth one suffers so much; and parting from my mother was any time a sufficient grief. In those days railways were not numerous, and I had to journey a good way by coach. About eleven at night I found myself at my destination. At the door a maid-servant appeared; no one else: it was scarcely to be expected by "the governess." This was a new and sad "coming home" to me. I was shown to my bedroom, hearing, as I passed the landing, much rustling of dresses and "squittling" away of little feet—(I ought to apologise for that odd expression, which, I think, I learned when I was quite a child, and used to go angling with my father and Mr. Sutherland. It means a scampering off in all directions, as a shoal of minnows do when you throw a pebble among them). I asked if the family were gone to bed, and was informed, "No;" so I arranged my dress and went downstairs, unconsciously reassured by the fact that the house was neither so large nor so aristocratic as my very liberal salary had at first inclined me to expect.

"Who shall I say, miss?" asked the rather untidy servant, meeting me in the lobby, and staring with open eyes, as if a stranger were some rare sight. "Miss Pryor," I said, thinking regretfully that I should be henceforth that, and not "Cassia;"

and seeing the maid still stared, I added with an effort, "I am the new governess." So under that double announcement I appeared at the parlour-door. The room was rather dark: there were two candles, but one had been extinguished, and was being hurriedly relighted as I entered. At first I saw nothing clearly; then I perceived a little pale lady sitting at one end of the table, and two half-grown-up girls, dressed in "going-out-to-tea" costume, seated primly together on the sofa. There was a third; but she vanished out of the door as I entered it.

"Miss Pryor, I believe?" said a timid voice—so timid that I could hardly believe that it was a lady addressing her governess. I glanced at her: she was a little woman, with pale hair and light eyes—frightened-looking eyes—that just rose, and fell in a minute. I said "I was Miss Pryor, and concluded I addressed Mrs. Le Poer." She answered "Yes, yes," and held out hesitatingly a thin, cold, bird-like hand, which I took rather warmly than otherwise; for I felt really sorry for her evident nervousness. It seemed so strange for any one to be afraid of *me*. "My daughters, Miss Pryor," she then said in a louder tone. Whereupon the two girls rose, curtsied, blushed—seemingly more from awkwardness than modesty—and sat down again. I shook hands with both, trying to take the initiative, and make myself sociable and at home—a difficult matter, my position feeling much like that of a fly in an ice-house.

"These are my pupils, then?" said I cheerfully. "Which is Miss Zillah?"—for I remembered Mr. Sutherland had mentioned that name in his letter, and its peculiarity naturally struck me.

The mother and daughters looked rather blankly at each other, and the former said, "This is Miss Le Poer and Miss Matilda; Zillah is not in the room at present."

"Oh, a third sister?" I observed.

"No, ma'am," rather pertly answered Miss Le Poer; "Zill is not our sister at all, but only a sort of a distant relation of Pa's, whom he is very kind to and keeps at his expense; and who mends our stockings and brushes our hair of nights, and whom we are very kind to also."

"Oh, indeed!" was all I said in reply to this running stream of very provincially spoken and unpunctuated English. I was rather puzzled too; for if my memory was correct—and I generally remembered Mr. Sutherland's letters very clearly, probably because they were themselves so clear—he had particularly mentioned my future pupil, Zillah Le Poer, and no Miss Le Poer besides. I waited with some curiosity for the girl's reappearance;

at last I ventured to say, "I should like to see Miss Zillah. I understood"—here I hesitated, but thought afterwards that plain speech was best—"I understood from Mr. Sutherland that she was to be my pupil."

"Of course, of course," hastily said the lady, and I fancied she coloured slightly. "Caroline, fetch your cousin."

Caroline sulkily went out, and shortly returned followed by a girl older than herself, though clad in childish, or rather servant fashion, with short petticoats, short sleeves, and a big brown-holland pinafore.[1] "Zill wouldn't stay to be dressed," explained Caroline in a loud whisper to her mother; at which Mrs. Le Poer looked more nervous and uncomfortable than ever. Meanwhile I observed my pupil. I had fancied the Zillah so carefully entrusted to my care by Mr. Sutherland to be a grown young lady, who only wanted "finishing." I even thought she might be a beauty. With some surprise I found her a half-caste girl—with an olive complexion, full Hindu[2] lips, and eyes very black and bright. She was untidily dressed, which looked the worse, since she was almost a woman; though her dull, heavy face had the stupidity of an ultra-stupid child. I saw all this; for somehow—probably because I had heard of her before—I examined the girl more than I did the two other Misses Le Poer. Zillah herself stared at me much as if I had been a wild animal, and then put her finger in her mouth with a babyish air. "How do you do, my dear?" said I desperately, feeling that all four pair of family-eyes were upon me. "I hope we shall be good friends soon." And I put out my hand. At first the girl seemed not to understand that I meant to shake hands with her. Then she irresolutely poked out her brown fingers, having first taken the precaution to wipe them on her pinafore. I made another remark or two about my being her governess, and her studying with her cousins; at which she opened her large eyes with a dull amaze, but I never heard the sound of her voice.

It must have been now near twelve o'clock. I thought it odd the girls should be kept up so late, and began at last to speculate whether I was to see Mr. Le Poer. My conjectures were soon set at rest by a loud pull at the door-bell, which made Mrs. Le Poer spring up from her chair, and Zillah vanish like lightning. The two others sat cowed, with their hands before them; and I myself

---

1 Holland was an inexpensive linen fabric. Pinafores were worn over dresses and also used as protective aprons.

2 The 1897 text replaces "Hindoo" (used in the 1851, 1853, and 1859 texts) with "Hindu."

felt none of the bravest. So upon this frightened group the master of the house walked in.

"Hollo, Mrs. Le Poer! Carry! Zill, you fool! Confound it, where's the supper?" (*I* might have asked that too, being very hungry.) "What the deuce are you all about?"

"My dear!" whispered the wife beseechingly, as she met him at the door, and seemed pointing to me.

Certainly I could not have believed that the voice just heard belonged to the gentleman who now entered. The *gentleman*, I repeat; for I never saw one who more thoroughly looked the character. He was about fifty, very handsome, very well dressed—his whole mien bespeaking that stately, gracious courtliness which now, except in rare instances, belongs to a past age. Bowing, he examined me curiously, with a look that somehow or other made me uncomfortable. He seemed viewing over my feminine attractions as a horse-dealer does the points of a new bargain. But soon the interest of the look died away. I knew he considered me as all others did—a very plain and shy young woman, perhaps lady-like (I believe I was that, for I heard of some one saying so), but nothing more. "I have the pleasure of meeting Miss Pryor?" said he in an ultra-bland tone, which after his first coarse manner would have positively startled me, had I not always noticed that the two are often combined in the same individual. (I always distrust a man who speaks in a very mild, measured, womanish voice.) I mentioned the name of his friend Mr. Sutherland. "Oh, I recollect," said he stiffly: "Mr. Sutherland informed you that—that——" He evidently wished to find out exactly what I knew of himself and his family. Now, it being always my habit to speak the plain truth, I saw no reason why I should not gratify him; so I stated the simple facts of our friend's letter to my mother—that he had found for me a situation in the family of a Mr. Le Poer, and had particularly charged me with completing the education of Miss Zillah Le Poer. "Oh!" said Mr. Le Poer abruptly; "were those all your instructions, my dear Miss Pryor?" he added insinuatingly. I answered that I knew no more, having missed seeing Mr. Sutherland before I came away. "Then you come quite a stranger into my family? I hope you have received the hearty welcome a stranger should receive, and I trust you will soon cease to merit that name." So saying, he graciously touched the tips of my fingers, and in mellifluous tones ordered supper, gently reproaching his wife for having delayed that meal. "You know, my dear, it was needless to wait for me; and Miss Pryor must be needing refreshment."

Indeed I was so, being literally famished. The meal was ordinary enough—mere bread, butter, and cheese; but Mr. Le Poer did the honours with most gentlemanly courtesy. I thought, never did a poor governess meet with such attention. The girls did not sup with us: they had taken the earliest opportunity of disappearing; nor was the half-caste cousin again visible. We had soon done eating—that is, Mrs. Le Poer and I; for the gentleman seemed so indifferent to the very moderate attractions of his table, that from this fact, and from a certain redness of his eyes, I could not help suspecting he had well supped before. Still, that did not prevent his asking for wine; and having politely drunk with me, he composed himself to have a little confidential talk while he finished the decanter.

"Miss Pryor, do you correspond with Mr. Sutherland?"

The abruptness of his question startled me. I felt my cheeks tingling as I answered most truthfully, "No."

"Still, you are a dear and valued friend of his, he tells me."

I felt glad, so glad that I forgot to make the due answer about Mr. Sutherland's being "very kind."

My host had probably gained the information he wanted, and became communicative on his part. "I ought, my dear young lady, to explain a few things concerning your pupils, which have been thus accidentally omitted by my friend Mr. Sutherland, who could not better have acceded to my request than by sending a lady like yourself to instruct my family." Here he bowed and I bowed. We did a great deal in that way of dumb civility, as it saved him trouble and me words. "My daughters you have seen. They are, I believe, tolerably well-informed for such mere children." I wondered if I had rightly judged them at thirteen and fourteen. "My only trouble, Miss Pryor, is concerning my niece." Here I looked surprised, not suspecting Zillah to be so near a relative. "I call her niece through habit, and for the sake of her father, my poor deceased brother," continued Mr. Le Poer, with a lengthened and martyr-like visage; "but in truth she has no real claim to belong to my family. My brother—sad fellow always—Indian life not over-scrupulous—ties between natives and Europeans; in fact, my dear Miss Pryor, Zillah's mother—— You understand?" Ignorant as I was, I did dimly understand, coloured deeply, and was silent. In the unpleasant pause which ensued, I noticed that Mrs. Le Poer had let her knitting fall, and sat gazing on her husband with a blank, horrified look, until he called her to order by an impressive "A little more wine, my dear?" Her head sank with an alarmed gesture, and her lord and master continued addressing me. "Of course, this explanation is in strict confidence. Regard for my brother's memory induces me to keep the secret, and to bring up this girl exactly as my own—except," he added, himself, "with a slight, indeed a necessary difference. Therefore you will educate them all alike; at least so far as Zillah's small capacity allows. I believe"—and he smiled sarcastically—"her modicum of intellect is not greater than generally belongs to her mother's race. She would make an excellent *ayah*,[1] and that is all."

"Poor thing!" I thought, not inclined to despise her even after this information; how could I, when—— Now that fairly nonplussed me: what made the girl an object of interest to Mr. Sutherland? and why did he mention her as Miss Zillah Le Poer when she could legally have no right to the name? I should, in my straightforward way, have asked the question, but Mr. Le Poer's manner showed that he wished no more conversation. He hinted something about my fatigue, and the advisability of retiring; nay, even lighted my candle for me, and dismissed his wife and myself with an air so pleasant and gracious that I thought I had scarcely ever seen such a perfect gentleman.

Mrs. Le Poer preceded me upstairs to my room, bade me good-night, asked timidly, but kindly, if all was to my liking, and if I would take anything more—seemed half-inclined to say something else, and then, hearing her husband's voice, instantaneously disappeared.

I was at last alone. I sat thinking over this strange evening—so strange that it kept my thoughts from immediately flying where I had supposed they were sure to fly. During my cogitations there came a knock to the door, and on my answering it a voice spoke without, in a dull, sullen tone, and an accent slightly foreign and broken: "Please, do you want to be called to-morrow, and will you have any hot water?" I opened the door at once to Zillah. "Is it you, my dear? Come in and say good-night to me." The girl entered with the air and manner of a servant, except for a certain desperate sullenness. I took her hand, and thanked her for coming to see after my comforts. She looked thoroughly astonished; but still, as I went on talking, began to watch me with more interest. Once she even smiled, which threw a soft expression over her mouth. I cannot tell what reason I had—whether from a mere impulse of kindness, with which my own state of desolation had something to do, or whether I compelled myself from a sense

1 An Indian children's nurse or housemaid.

of duty to take all means of making a good first impression on the girl's feelings—but when I bade Zillah good-night I leant forward and just touched her brown cheek with mine—French fashion: for I could not really *kiss* anybody except for love. I never saw a creature so utterly amazed! She might have never received that token of affection since her birth. She muttered a few unintelligible words—I fancy they were in Hindustanee—flung herself before me, Eastern fashion, and my poor hand was kissed passionately, weepingly, as the beloved ladies' hands are in novels and romances. But mine was never kissed save by this poor child! All passed in a moment, and I had hardly recovered my first surprise when Zillah was gone. I sat a little while, feeling as strange as if I had suddenly become the heroine of a fairy tale; then caught a vision of my own known self, with my pale, tired face and sad-coloured gown. It soon brought me back to the realities of life, and to the fact that I was now two hundred miles away from my mother and from—London.

I had not been three weeks resident in the Le Poer family before I discovered that if out of the domestic mysteries into which I became gradually initiated I could create any fairy tale, it would certainly be that of "Cinderella;" but my poor Cinderella had all the troubles of her prototype without any of the graces either of mind or person. It is a great mistake to suppose that every victim of tyranny must of necessity be an angel. On most qualities of mind oppression has exactly the opposite effect. It dulls the faculties, stupefies the instinctive sense of right and makes the most awful havoc among the natural affections. I was often forced to doubt whether Mr. Le Poer was very far wrong when he called Zillah by his favourite name of the "ugly little devil." There was something quite demoniac in her black eyes at times. She was lazy, too—full of the languor of her native clime. Neither threats nor punishments could rouse her into the slightest activity. The only person to whom she paid the least attention was Mrs. Le Poer, who alone never ill-used her. Poor lady! she was too broken-spirited to ill-use anybody; but she never praised. I do not think Zillah had heard the common civility, "Thank you," until I came into the house; since, when I uttered it, she seemed scarcely to believe her ears. When she first joined us in the school-room I found the girl was very ignorant. Her youngest cousin was far before her even in the commonest knowledge; and, as in all cases of deadened intellect, it cost her incalculable trouble to learn the simplest things. I took infinite pains with her; ay, and felt in her a strong interest too—ten times stronger than in the other two; yet for weeks she seemed scarcely to have advanced at all. To be sure, it must be taken into account that she was rarely suffered to remain with me half the school-hours without being summoned to some menial duty or other; and the one maid-servant bestowed on me many black looks, as being the cause why she herself had sometimes to do a morning's household work alone. Often I puzzled myself in seeing how strangely incompatible was Zillah's position with Mr. Sutherland's expressed desire concerning her. Sometimes I thought I would write and explain all to him; but I did not like. Nor did I tell my mother half the *désagréments*[1] and odd things belonging to this family—considering that such reticence even towards her nearest kindred is every governess's duty. In all domestic circles there must be some secrets which chance observers should strictly keep.[2]

More than once I determined to take advantage of the very polite and sociable terms which Mr. Le Poer and myself were on, to speak to him on the subject, and argue that his benevolence in adopting his brother's unfortunate child might not suffer by being testified in a more complete and gracious form. But he was so little at home—and no wonder; for the miserably dull, secluded, and painfully economical way in which they lived could have little charms for a man of fashion and talent, or at least the relics of such, which he evidently was. And so agreeable as he could be! His conversation at meals—the only time I ever saw him—was a positive relief from the dull blank, broken only by the girls' squabbles, and their mother's faint remonstrances and complaints. But whenever, by dint of great courage, I contrived to bring Zillah's name on the tapis,[3] he always so adroitly crept out of the subject, without pointedly changing it, that afterwards I used to wonder how I had contrived to forget my purpose and leave matters as they were. The next scheme I tried was one which, in many family jars and family bitternesses among which my calling has placed me, I have found to answer amazingly well. It is my maxim that "a wrong is seldom a one-sided wrong;" and when you cannot amend one party, the next best thing is to try the other. I always had a doctrine likewise, that it is only those

1 Unpleasantnesses (French).

2 The 1851, 1853, and 1859 texts have "In all domestic circles there must be a little Eleusinia, the secrets of which chance observers should strictly keep."

3 Carpet (French); on the table, under consideration.

who have the instinct and the sins of servitude who will hopelessly remain oppressed. I determined to try if there was anything in Zillah's mind or disposition that could be awakened, so as to render her worthy of a higher position than that she held. And as my firm belief is, that everything and everybody in time rise or sink to their own proper level, so I felt convinced that if there were any superiority in Zillah's character, all the tyranny in the world would not keep her the pitiable Cinderella of such ordinary people as the Le Poers. I began my system by teaching her, not in public, where she was exposed to the silent but not less apparent contempt of her cousins, but at night in my own room, after all the house had retired. I made this hour as little like lessons as possible, by letting her sit and work with me, or brush my hair, teaching her orally the while. As much as her reserve permitted, I lured her into conversation on every indifferent subject. All I wanted was to get at the girl's heart. One day I was lecturing her in a quiet way on the subject concerning which she was the first young woman I ever knew that needed lecturing—care over her personal appearance. She certainly was the most slovenly girl I ever saw. Poor thing! she had many excuses; for, though the whole family dressed shabbily, and, worse, tawdrily, her clothes were the worst of all. Still, nothing but positive rags can excuse a woman for neglecting womanly neatness. I often urged despairingly upon poor Zillah that the meanest frock was no apology for untidy hair; that the most unpleasant work did not exclude the possibility of making face and hands clean after it was over. "Look at yours, my dear," said I once, taking the reluctant fingers and spreading them out on mine. Then I saw what I have often noticed in the Hindu race, how delicate her hands were naturally, even despite her hard servant's work. I told her so; for in a creature so crushed there was little fear of vanity, and I made it a point to praise her every good quality, personal and mental.

Zillah looked pleased. "My hands are like my mother's, who was very handsome, and a Parsee."[1]

"Do you remember her?"

"A little—not much and chiefly her hands, which were covered with rings. One, a great diamond, was worth ever so many hundred rupees.[2] It was lost once, and my mother cried. I saw it, a good while after, on my father's finger when he was dying,"

---

1 Members of the Parsi community follow the Zoroastrian religion and trace their ethnic roots to Persia.

2 The common currency of India.

continued she carelessly; and afterwards added mysteriously, "I think he stole it."

"Hush, child! hush! It is wrong to speak so of a dead father," cried I, much shocked.

"Is it? Well, I'll not do it if it vexes you, Miss Pryor."

This seemed her only consciousness of right or wrong—pleasing or displeasing me. At all events it argued well for my influence over her and her power of being guided by the affections. I asked again about her father; somehow, with a feminine prejudice, natural though scarcely right, I felt a delicacy in mentioning the mother. But she was the only parent of whom Zillah would speak. "I hardly know," "I can't remember," "I don't care," were all the answers my questions won. "You saw your father when he was dying?" I persisted. "An awful sight it must have been." Zillah shuddered at the recollection. "What did he say to you?"

"I don't remember, except that I was like my mother. All the rest was swearing, as uncle swears at me. But uncle did not do it then."

"So Mr. Le Poer was present?"

"Yes; and the ugly, horrible-looking man they said was my father talked to him in whispers, and Uncle took me on his knee and called me 'My dear.' He never did it afterwards."

I asked her one question more—"How long was this ago?" and she said, "Several years; she did not recollect how many."

I talked to her no more that night, but bade her go to rest. In fact, my mind was so full of her that I was glad to get her visible self out of the way. She went, lazily and stupidly as ever. Only at the door she paused. "You won't tell what I have been saying, Miss Pryor? You'll not mention my mother before them? I did once, and they laughed and made game of her, uncle and all. They did—they——" She stopped, literally foaming at the mouth with rage.

"Come in again; do, my poor child," said I, gently approaching. But she shut the door hurriedly and ran downstairs to the kitchen, where she slept with her dire enemy, yet sole companion, the servant-maid.

Six months after my coming to the Le Poers I began heartily to wish for some of my salary; not that I had any doubt of it—Mr. Sutherland had said it was sure—but I wanted some replenishment of my wardrobe, and, besides, it was near my mother's birthday, when I always took care she had some nice, useful gift. It quite puzzled me to think what little luxury she wanted, for she wrote me word Mr. Sutherland brought her so many. "He was just like a son to her," she said. Ah me! One day, when disconsolately examining my last pair of boots—the "wee boots," that, for a foolish reason I had, were one of my few feminine vanities—I took courage to go downstairs and ask Mr. Le Poer "if he could make it convenient," &c. "My dear Miss Pryor," said he, with most gentlemanly *empressement*,[1] "if I had thought—indeed you should have asked me before. Let me see; you have been here six months, and our stipulated sum was——" I thought he hesitated on account of the delicacy some gentlemen feel in business dealings with a lady; indeed I supposed it was from that cause he had never spoken to me about money matters. However, I felt no such delicacy, but answered plainly, "My salary, Mr. Sutherland said, was to be a hundred guineas a year." "Exactly so; and payable yearly, I believe?" Mr. Le Poer added carelessly. Now, I had not remembered that, but of course he knew. However, I looked and felt disappointed. At last, as Mr. Le Poer spoke with the kindest politeness, I confessed the fact that I wanted the money for habiliments.[2] "Oh, is that all? Then pray, my excellent young lady, go with Caroline to town at once.[3] Order anything you like of my trades-people. Bid them put all to my account: we can settle afterwards. No excuses; indeed you must." He bowed me away with the air of a benefactor disdaining gratitude, and set off immediately on one of his frequent jaunts. There was no help for it; so I accepted his plan, and went to town with Caroline and Matilda.

It seemed a long time since I had been in any town, and the girls might never have been there in their lives, so eagerly did they linger at shop-windows, admiring and longing after finery. The younger consoled the elder, saying that they would have all these sort of grand things some time. "It's only four years," whispered she—"just four years, and then that stupid Zill——" Here Caroline pushed her back with an angry "Hush!" and walked up to my side with a prim smile. I thought it strange, but took no notice, always disliking to play the governess out of school-hours.

Another odd thing happened the same week. There came a letter to Mr. Le Poer from Mr. Sutherland. I could not help noticing this, as it lay on the mantel-shelf two days before the former returned, and I used to see it always when I sat at meals.

---

1 Eagerness or effusion (French).

2 Clothing.

3 The 1851, 1853, and 1859 texts have "H—," in place of "town."

His—Mr. Sutherland's I mean—was a fair, large hand, too, which would have caught any one's eye; it was like old times to see it again. I happened to be by when Mr. Le Poer opened the letter. He was so anxious over it that he did not notice my presence. Perhaps it was wrong of me to glance toward him, but yet natural, considering it was a friend's letter. I saw a little note enclosed, the address of which, I was almost sure, bore my own name. I waited, thinking he would give it me. I even made some slight movement to attract his attention. He looked up—he actually started—but next moment smiled as only Mr. Le Poer could smile. "News from our friend, you see," said he, showing me the outside envelope. "He is quite well, and—let me consider"—glancing over his own letter—"he sends his kindest remembrances to you. A most worthy man is Mr. Sutherland." So saying, he folded the epistle and placed it in his desk. The little note, which he had turned seal uppermost, he quietly put, unopened, into his pocket. It must have been my own delusion, then. Not the first, nor yet the last!

At the expiration of my first year as a governess, just as I was looking with untold eagerness to my midsummer holidays, when I was at length to go home to my mother—for the journey to London was too expensive to admit of that happiness more than once a year—there happened a great disaster to the Le Poer family: no less than that terrible scourge, typhus fever.[1] Matilda took it first, then Caroline, then the mother. These three were scarcely convalescent when Zillah caught the fever in her turn, and had it more dangerously than any of the rest. Her life was in danger for many days, during which I had the sole anxiety and responsibility; for Mr. Le Poer, on the first tidings of the fever, had taken flight, and been visible at home no more. True, he wrote every other day most touching letters, and I in return kept him constantly informed as to the progress of his wife and children. When Zillah was taken ill, however, I did not think it necessary to send him word concerning her, feeling that the poor orphan's life was precious to no one. I never was more surprised than when, on Mr. Le Poer's venturing back and finding Zillah in the crisis of her disease, his terror and anxiety appeared uncontrollable. "Good God!" he cried, "Zillah ill? Zillah going to die?

1 Typically transferred by lice, typhus fever was particularly feared in the nineteenth century, as several major epidemics occurred. In 1847–48, immediately prior to Craik's writing *The Half-Caste*, a major epidemic killed thousands of people in Ireland, Scotland, and England. A reliable vaccine was not developed until the mid-twentieth century.

Impossible! Why was I not informed before? Confound you, madam"—and he turned furiously to his still ailing wife—"did you not think? Are you mad—quite mad?"

I declare I thought *he* was. Mrs. Le Poer only sobbed in silence. Meanwhile the outcries of the delirious girl were heard in the very parlour. I had given her my room; I thought, poor soul, she should not die in her damp kitchen-closet.

Mr. Le Poer turned absolutely white with terror—he, who had expressed only mild concern when his wife and daughters were in peril. "Miss Pryor," said he hoarsely, "something must be done. That girl *must* be saved; I'd snatch her from the very fiend himself! Send for advice, physicians, nurses; send to Leeds, Liverpool—to London even. Only, by ——, she must not die!"

Poor Zillah did not die. She was saved for Heaven's strange purposes; though I, in my then blindness, often and often, while sitting by her bed-side, thought it would be better did she slip quietly out of the bitter world in which she seemed to be only an unsightly and trampled weed. Mr. Le Poer's unwonted anxiety did not end with her convalescence, which was very slow. "She may die yet!" I heard him muttering to himself the first day after he saw his niece. "Miss Pryor, my wife is a foo— I mean, a rather undecided person. Tell me what you think ought to be done for Zillah's recovery." I prescribed, but with little hope that my advice would be followed—immediate change to sea air. "It shall be done!" at once said he. "Mrs. Le Poer and the girls can take care of her; or stay—she likes you best. Miss Pryor, are you willing to go?"

This question perfectly confounded me. I had been so longingly anticipating my going home—delayed, as in common charity I could not but delay it, on account of the fever. Now this trouble was over I had quite counted on my departure. That very week I had been preparing my small wardrobe, so as to look as nice as possible in my mother's eyes. She had given me a hint to do so, since she and I were to spend the vacation together at Mr. Sutherland's country-house, and old Mrs. Sutherland was so very particular. "Why do you hesitate?" said Mr. Le Poer rather sharply. "Are you thinking of the money? You shall have any additional salary—£50 more if you choose. Upon my soul, madam, you shall!—only I entreat you to go." I would not have minded his entreaties, but I was touched by those of Zillah, who seemed terrified at the idea of going to a strange place without me. Then, too, the additional money, not unneeded; for Mr. Sutherland, so kindly generous in other things, had the still rarer generosity never to offer us *that*. I determined to write and tell my mother the position of affairs. Her good judgment would decide; or if hers failed, she would be sure to appeal to her trusty and only adviser since my father died; and I was content to abide by *his* decision. He did decide. He told my mother that it was his earnest wish I should stay a little longer with Zillah Le Poer, whom he called "his ward." Her history, he said, he would inform me of when we met, which must be ere long, as he was contemplating returning to India for some years.

Mr. Sutherland returning to India! And before his departure he must see me—*me!* It was a very simple and natural thing, as I felt afterwards, but not then. I did what he desired—as indeed I had long been in the habit of doing—and accompanied Zillah.

I had supposed that we should go to some near watering-place, or at all events the Liverpool shore. Indeed I had pointedly recommended Tranmere, where, as I stated to Mr. Le Poer, there was living an aunt of Mr. Sutherland's, who would have taken lodgings or done anything in her power for her nephew's ward. To my surprise, he gently objected to this plan. After staying a night in Liverpool, instead of crossing to the opposite shore, as I expected, he put us all—that is, Zillah, the two other girls, and myself—on board the Belfast boat, and there we found ourselves floating across the Irish Channel! The two Misses Le Poer were considerably frightened; Zillah looked most happy. She said it reminded her of her voyage to England when she was a little child. She had never seen the sea since. Long after we got out of sight of land she and I sat together on the deck in the calm summer evening, talking of this Indian voyage, and what it was like, and what people did during the long four months from land to land. She gave me much information, to which I listened with strange interest. I well remember—fool that I was!—sitting on the deck of that Belfast boat, with the sun dipping into the sea before us, and the moon rising on the other side—sitting and thinking what it would be to feel one's self on the deck of some Indian-bound ship, alone, or else in companionship that might make the word still correct, according to its original reading—*all one*: an etymological notion worthy of a governess!

The only remarkable event of our voyage was my sudden introduction by Mr. Le Poer to a personage whom I had not thought existed. "My son, Miss Pryor; my eldest and only son, Lieutenant Augustus Le Poer." I was very considerably surprised, as I had never heard of the young gentleman. I could only hurriedly conjecture, what I afterwards found to be the truth, that this was the son of a former marriage, and that there had been some family quarrel, lately healed. The lieutenant bowed to me, and I to him. Zillah, who sat by me, had no share in the introduction, until the young man, sticking his glass[1] into his eye, stared at her energetically, muttering to his father some question, in which I just detected the words, "odd fish." "Only Zillah," answered Mr. Le Poer carelessly. "Child, this is your cousin Augustus, lately returned from foreign service. Shake hands with him." Zillah listlessly obeyed; but her "cousin" seemed not at all to relish the title. He cast his eyes superciliously over her. I must confess my poor child's appearance was not very attractive. I did not wonder that Lieutenant Augustus merely nodded his head, twirled his moustache, and walked away. Zillah just looked lazily after him, and then her eyes declined upon the beautiful expanse of sea.

For my part, I watched our new friend with some curiosity and amusement, especially when Caroline and Matilda appeared, trying to do the agreeable. The lieutenant was to them evidently the *beau-ideal*[2] of a brother. For myself, I did not admire him at all. Unluckily, if I have three positive aversions in the world, it is for dandies, men with moustaches, and soldiers—and he was a compound of all three. Also, he was a small man; and I, like most little women, have a great reverence for height in the other sex—not universally, for some of my truest friends have been diminutive men—excellent, worthy, admirable Zaccheuses.[3] Still, from an ancient prejudice, acquired—no matter how—my first impression of any man is usually in proportion to his inches; therefore Lieutenant Le Poer did not stand very high in my estimation.

Little notice did he condescend to take of us, which was rather a satisfaction than otherwise; but he soon became very fraternal and confidential with his two sisters. I saw them all chattering together until it grew dusk; and long after that, the night being fine, I watched their dark figures walking up and down the other side of the deck. More than once I heard their laughter, and detected in their talk the name of Zillah; so I supposed the girls were ridiculing her to their brother. Poor child! she was fast asleep, with her head on my shoulder, wrapped closely up, so that

1 A monocle or magnifying glass usually hanging from a chain or ribbon attached to a piece of clothing.

2 Beautiful ideal (French); an ideal type or model.

3 Zacchaeus is the short-statured tax collector mentioned in Luke 19:1–10.

the mild night could do her no harm. She looked almost pretty—the light of the August moon so spiritualised her face. I felt thankful she had not died, but that, under Heaven, my care had saved her—for what? Ay, for what? If, as I kissed the child, I had then known—— But no, I should have kissed her still!

Our brief voyage ended, we reached Belfast and proceeded to Holywood—a small sea-bathing village a few miles down the coast. To this day I have never found out why Mr. Le Poer took the trouble to bring us all over the water and settle us there, as it was so dull and dreary that, to all intents and purposes, we might as well have been buried in the solitudes of the Desert of Sahara.[1] But perhaps that was exactly what he wanted.

I think that never in her life, at least since childhood, could Zillah have been so happy as she was during the first week or two of our sojourn at Holywood. To me, who in my youth, when we were rich and could travel, had seen much beautiful scenery, the place was rather uninteresting; to her it was perfection! As she grew stronger life seemed to return to her again under quite a new aspect. To be sure, it was a great change in her existence to have no one over her but me—for her uncle and cousin Augustus had of course speedily vanished from this quiet spot—to be able to do just what she liked, which was usually nothing at all. She certainly was not made for activity; she would lie whole days on the beach, or on the grassy walk which came down to the very edge of high-water-mark—covering her eyes with her poke-bonnet,[2] or gazing sleepily from under her black lashes at the smooth loch, and the wavy line of hills on the opposite shore. Matilda and Caroline ran very wild too: since we had no lessons, I found it hard work to make them obey me at all; indeed it was always a great pain for a quiet soul like me to have to assume authority. I should have got on better even with Mrs. Le Poer to assist me; but she, poor little woman, terrified at change, had preferred staying quietly at home in Yorkshire. I was not quite sure but that she had the best of it after all.

In the course of a week my cares were somewhat lightened. The lieutenant reappeared, and from that time forward I had very little of the girls' company. He was certainly a kind brother; I could not but acknowledge that. He took them about a great deal, or else stayed at Holywood, leaving us by the late evening

---

1 The 1851, 1853, and 1859 texts omit "as it was so dull and dreary."

2 A woman's hat with a wide, rounded front brim also known as a Neapolitan bonnet.

train, as he said, to go to his lodgings at Belfast. I, the temporary mistress of the establishment, was of course quite polite to my pupils' brother, and he was really very civil to me, though he treated me with the distance due to an ancient duenna.[1] This amused me sometimes, seeing I was only twenty-six—probably his own age; but I was always used to be regarded as an old maid. Of Zillah the lieutenant hardly ever took any notice at all, and she seemed to keep out of his way as much as possible. When he left us in the evening—and there was always a tolerable confusion at that time, his two sisters wanting to see him off by the train, which he never by any chance allowed—then came the quietest and pleasantest half-hour of the day. The Misses Le Poer disliked twilight rambles, so Zillah and I always set off together. Though oftentimes we parted company, and I was left sitting on the beach, while she strolled on to a pleasant walk she said she had found—a deserted house, whose grounds sloped down to the very shore. But I, not very strong then, and weighed down by many anxious thoughts, loved better to sit and stupefy myself with the murmur of the sea—a habit not good for me, but pleasant. No fear had I of Zillah's losing herself, or coming to any harm; and the girl seemed so happy in her solitary rambles that I had not the desire to stop them, knowing how a habit of self-dependence is the greatest comfort to a woman, especially to one in her desolate position. But though, as her nature woke up and her dulness was melting away, Zillah seemed more *self-contained*, so to speak; more reserved, and relying on her own thoughts for occupation and amusement, still she had never been so attentive or affectionate to me. It was a curious and interesting study—this young mind's unfolding, though I regret to say that just then I did not think about Zillah as much as I ought to have done. Often I reproached myself for this afterwards; but as things turned out, I now feel, with a quiet self-compassion, that my error was pardonable.

I mind one evening—now *I mind* is not quite English, but I learned it, with other Scottish phrases, in my young days, so let it stand!—I mind one evening that, being not quite in a mood to keep my own company, I went out walking with Zillah; somehow the noise of the sea wearied me, and unconsciously I turned through the village and along the high-road—almost like an English road, so beautiful with overhanging trees. I did not talk much, and Zillah walked quite silently, which indeed was

1 An older Spanish woman who acts as a chaperone.

nothing new. I think I see her now, floating along with her thin but lithe figure and limp, clinging dress—the very antipodes of fashion—nothing about her that would really be called beautiful except her great eyes, that were perfect oceans of light. When we came to a gateway—which, like most things in poor Ireland, seemed either broken down or left half finished—she looked round rather anxiously.

"Do you know this, my dear?"

"It is an old mansion—a place I often like to stroll in."

"What! have you been there alone?"

"Of course I have," said she quickly, and slightly colouring. "You knew it; or I thought you did."

She appeared apprehensive of reproof, which struck me as odd in so inoffensive a matter, especially as I was anything but a cross governess. To please and reassure her I said, "Well, never mind, my dear; you shall show me your pet paradise. It will be quite a treat."

"I don't think so, Miss Pryor. It's all weeds and disorder, and you can't endure that. And the ground is very wet here and there. I am sure you'll not like it at all."

"Oh, but I will, if only to please you, Zillah," said I, determined to be at once firm and pacific—for I saw a trace of her old sullen look troubling my pupil's face, as if she did not like her haunts to be intruded upon even by me. However, she made no more open opposition, and we entered the grounds, which were almost English in their aspect, except in one thing—their entire desolation. The house might not have been inhabited, or the grounds cultivated, for twenty years. The rose-beds grew wild, great patches of white clover overspread the lawn and flower-garden, and all the underwood was one mass of tall fern.

I had not gone far in and out of the tangled walks of the shrubbery when I found that Zillah had slipped away. I saw her at a distance standing under a tall Portugal laurel seemingly doing nothing but meditate—a new occupation for her; so I left her to it, and penetrated deeper in what my old French governess would have called the *bocage*.[1] My feet sank deep in fern, amidst which I plunged, trying to gather a great armful of that and of wild-flowers; for I had, and have still, the babyish propensity of wishing to pluck everything I see, and never can conquer the delight I feel in losing myself in a wilderness of vegetation. In that oblivion of child-like content I was happy—happier than I had

1 Wooded area (French).

been for a long time. The ferns nearly hid me, when I heard a stirring in the bushes behind, which I took for some harmless animal that I had disturbed. However, hares, foxes, or even squirrels do not usually give a loud "Ahem!" in the perfectly human tone which followed. At first I had terrors of some stray keeper, who might possibly shoot me for a rabbit or a poacher, till I recollected that I was not in England but in Ireland, where unjust landlords are regarded as the more convenient game.

"Ahem!" reiterated the mysterious voice—"ahem! Is it you, my angel?" Never could any poor governess be more thoroughly dumfounded. Of course the adjective was not meant for me. Impossible! Still, it was unpleasant to come into such near contact with a case of philandering. Mere philandering it must be, for this was no village-tryst, the man's accent being refined and quite English. Besides, little as I knew of love-making, it struck me that in any serious attachment people would never address one another by the silly title of "my angel." It must be some idle flirtation going on among the strolling visitants whom we occasionally met on the beach, and who had probably wandered up through the gate which led to these grounds. To put an end to any more confidential disclosures from this unseen gentleman, I likewise said "Ahem!" as loud as I could, and immediately called out for Zillah. Whereupon there was a hasty rustling in the bushes, which, however, soon subsided, and the place became quite still again, without my ever having caught sight of the very complimentary individual who had in this extempore manner addressed me as his "angel." "Certainly," I thought, "I must have been as invisible to him as he to me, or he never would have done it."

Zillah joined me quickly. She looked half frightened, and said she feared something was the matter: had I seen anything? At first I was on the point of telling her all, but somehow it now appeared a rather ridiculous position for a governess to be placed in—to have shouted for assistance on being addressed by mistake by an unknown admirer; and, besides, I did not wish to put any love-notions into the girl's head: they come quite soon enough of their own accord. So I merely said I had been startled by hearing voices in the bushes—that perhaps we were intruders on the domain, and had better not stay longer. "Yet the place seems quite retired and desolate," said I to Zillah as we walked down the tangled walk that led to the beach, she evidently rather unwilling to go home. "Do you ever meet any strangers about here?"

She answered briefly, "No."

"Did you see any one to-night?"
"Yes"—given with a slight hesitation.
"Who was it?"
"A man, I think—at a distance."
"Did he speak to you?"
"No."

I give these questions and answers verbatim, to show—what I believed then, and believe now—that, so far as I questioned, Zillah answered truthfully. I should be very sorry to think that either at that time or any other she had told me a wilful lie. But this adventure left an uncomfortable sensation on my mind—not from any doubt of Zillah herself, for I thought her still too much of a child, and, in plain words, too awkward and unattractive, to fear her engaging in love-affairs, clandestine or otherwise, for some time to come. Nevertheless, after this evening, I always contrived that we should take our twilight strolls in company, and that I should never lose sight of her for more than a few minutes together. Yet even with this precaution I proved to be a very simple and short-sighted governess after all.

We had been at Holywood a whole month, and I began to wonder when we should return home, as Zillah was quite well, indeed more blooming than I had ever seen her. Mr. Le Poer made himself visible once or twice, at rare intervals: he had always "business in Dublin," or "country visits to pay." His son acted as regent in his absence—I always supposed by his desire; nevertheless I often noticed that these two lights of the family never shone together, and the father's expected arrival was the signal of Mr. Augustus's non-appearance for some days. Nor did the girls ever allude to their brother. I thought family quarrels might perhaps have instructed them in this, and so was not surprised. It was certainly a relief to all when the head of the family again departed. We usually kept his letters for him, he not being very anxious about them, for which indifference, as I afterwards comprehended, he might have good reasons. Once there came a letter—I knew from whom—marked in the corner, "*If absent, to be opened by Miss Pryor.*" Greatly surprised was I to find it contained a bank-note, apparently hurriedly enclosed, with this brief line: "If Zillah requires more, let me know at once. She must have every luxury needful for her health.—A.S." The initials meant certainly his name—Andrew Sutherland; nor could I be mistaken in the hand. Yet it seemed very odd, as I had no idea that he held over her more than a nominal guardianship, just undertaken out of charity to the orphan, and from his having slightly known her father. At least so Mr. Le Poer told me. The only solution I could find was the simple one of this being a gift springing from the generosity of a heart whose goodness I knew but too well. However, to be quite sure, I called Caroline into counsel, thinking, silly as she was, she might know something of the matter. But she only tittered, looked mysteriously important, and would speak clearly on nothing, except that we had a perfect right to use the money—Pa always did; and that she wanted a new bonnet very badly indeed. A day or two after, Mr. Le Poer, returning unexpectedly, took the note into his own possession saying, smilingly, "that it was all right;" and I heard no more. But if I had not been the very simplest woman in the world I should have certainly suspected that things were not "all right." Nevertheless, I do not now wonder at my blindness. How could I think otherwise than well of a man whom I innocently supposed to be a friend of Mr. Sutherland?

"Zillah, my dear, do not look so disappointed. There is no help for it. Your uncle told me before he left us that we must go home next week." So said I, trying to say it gently, and not marvelling that the girl was unhappy at the near prospect of returning to her old miserable life. It was a future so bitter that I almost blamed myself for not having urged our longer stay. Still, human nature is weak, and I did so thirst for home—my own home. But it was hard that my pleasure should be the poor child's pain. "Don't cry, my love," I went on, seeing her eyes brimming and the colour coming and going in her face—strange changes which latterly, on the most trifling occasions, had disturbed the apparent stolidity of her manner. "Don't be unhappy; things may be smoother now; and I am sure your cousins behave better and kinder to you than they did. Even the lieutenant is very civil to you." A sparkle, which was either pleasure or pride, flashed from the girl's eyes, and then they drooped, unable to meet mine. "Be content, dear child; all may be happier than you expect. You must write to me regularly—you can write pretty well now, you know; you must tell me all that happens to you, and remember that in everything you can trust me entirely." Here I was astonished by Zillah's casting herself at my knees as I sat, and bursting into a storm of tears. Anxiously I asked her what was the matter.

"Nothing—everything! I am so happy—so wretched! Ah! what must I do?"

These words bubbled up brokenly from her lips, but just at that unlucky moment her three cousins came in. She sprang up like a frightened deer, and was off to her own room. I did not see her again all the afternoon, for Lieutenant Augustus kept me in the parlour on one excuse or another until I was heartily vexed at him and myself. When I went upstairs to put on my bonnet—we were all going to walk that evening—Zillah slipped away almost as soon as I appeared. I noticed that she was quite composed now, and had resumed her usual manner. I called after her to tell the two other girls to get ready, thinking it wisest to make no remarks concerning her excitement of the morning.

I never take long in dressing, and soon went down, rather quietly perhaps; for I was meditating with pain on how much this passionate child might yet have to suffer in the world. I believe I have rather a light step; at all events I was once told so. Certainly I did not intend to come into the parlour stealthily or pryingly; in fact, I never thought of its occupants at all. On entering, what was my amazement to see standing at the window—Lieutenant Augustus and—my Zillah! He was embracing—in plain English, kissing her. Now, I am no prude; I have sometimes known a harmless father-like or brother-like embrace pass between two, who, quite certain of each other's feelings, gave and received the same in all frankness and simplicity. But generally I am very particular, more so than most women. I often used to think that, were I a man, I would wish, in the sweet day of my betrothal, to know for certain that mine was the first *lover's* kiss ever pressed on the dear lips which I then sealed as wholly my own. But in this case, at one glance, even if I had not caught the silly phrase, "My angel!"—the same I heard in the wood (ah! that wood!)—I or any one would have detected the truth. It came upon me like a thunderbolt; but, knowing Zillah's disposition, I had just wit enough to glide back unseen and re-enter, talking loudly at the door. Upon which I found the lieutenant tapping his boots carelessly, and Zillah shrinking into a corner like a frightened hare. He went off very soon—he said, to an engagement at Belfast; and we started for our ramble. I noticed that Zillah walked alongside of Caroline, as if she could not approach or look at me.

I know not whether I was most shocked at her, or puzzled to think what possible attraction this young man could find in such a mere child—so plain and awkward-looking, too. That he could be "in love" with her, even in the lowest sense of that phrase, seemed all but an impossibility; and if not in love, what possible purpose could he have in wooing or wanting to marry her?—for I was simple enough to suppose that all wooing must necessarily be in earnest.

Half bewildered with conjectures, fears, and doubts as to what course I must pursue, I walked on beside Matilda, who, having quarrelled with her sister, kept close to me. She went chattering on about some misdoings of Caroline. At last my attention was caught by Zillah's name.

"I won't bear it always," said the angry child; "I'll only bear it till Zillah comes of age."

"Bear what?"

"Why, that Carry should always have two new frocks to my one. It's a shame!"

"But what has that to do with Zillah's coming of age?"

"Don't you know, Miss Pryor?—oh, of course you don't, for Carry wouldn't let me tell you; but I will!" she added maliciously.

I hardly knew whether I was right or wrong in not stopping the girl's tongue, but I could not do it.

"Do you know," she added in a sly whisper, "Carry says we shall all be very rich when Zillah comes of age. Pa and ma kept it very secret; but Carry found it out, and told it to brother Augustus and to me."

"Told what?" said I, forgetful that I was prying into a family secret, and stung into curiosity by the mention of Augustus.

"That Zillah will then be very rich, as her father left her all he had; and uncle Henry was a great nabob,[1] because he married an Indian princess, and got all her money. Now, you see," she continued, with a cunning smile, shocking on that young face, "we must be very civil to Zillah, and of course she will give us all her money. Eh, you understand?"

I stood aghast. In a moment all came clear upon me: the secret of Mr. Sutherland's guardianship—of his letter to me intercepted—of the money lately sent—of Mr. Le Poer's anxiety concerning his niece's life—of his desire to keep her hidden from the world, lest she might wake to a knowledge of her position. The whole was a tissue of crimes. And—deepest crime of all!—I now guessed why Lieutenant Augustus wished, unknown to his father, to entrap her still childish affections, marry her, and secure all to himself. I never knew much of the world and its wickedness; I believed all men were like my father or Mr. Sutherland. This discovery for the time quite dizzied my faculties. I have not the slightest recollection of anything more that passed on that seaside walk, except that, coming in at the door of the cottage, I heard

1 An Anglo-Indian term for a British man who made his fortune in the East.

Zillah say in anxious tones, "What ails Miss Pryor, I wonder?" I had wisdom enough to answer, "Nothing, my dears!" and send them all to bed.

"Shall you be long after us?" asked Zillah, who, as I said, was my chamber-companion. "An hour or two," I replied, turning to the little parlour, trying to collect my thoughts. To any governess the discovery of a clandestine and unworthy love-affair among her pupils would be most painful, but my discoveries were all horror together. The more I thought it over, the more my agonised pity for Zillah overcame my grief at her deceitfulness. Love is always so weak, and girlish love at fifteen such a fascinating dream. Whatever I thought of the young lieutenant, he was very attractive to most people. He was, besides, the first man Zillah had ever known, and the first human being except myself who had treated her with kindness. He had done that from the first; but what other opportunities could they have had to become lovers? I recollected Zillah's wanderings, evening after evening, in the grounds of the deserted estate. She must have met him there. Poor girl! I could well imagine what it must be to be wooed under the glamour of summer twilight and beautiful solitude. No wonder Zillah's heart was stolen away! Thinking of this now, I feel I am wrong in saying "heart" of what at best could have been mere "fancy." Women's natures are different; but some natures I have known were gravely, mournfully, fatally in earnest, even at sixteen.

However, in earnest or not, she must be snatched from this marriage at all risks. There could be no doubt of that. But to whom should I apply for aid? Not to Mr. Le Poer, certainly. The poor orphan seemed trembling between the grasp of either villain, father and son. Whatever must be done for her I must do myself, of my own judgment, and on my own responsibility. It was a very hard strait for me. In my necessity I instinctively turned to my best friend in the world, and, as I suddenly remembered, Zillah's too. I determined to write and explain all to Mr. Sutherland. How well I remember that time! The little parlour quite still and quiet, except for the faint sound of the waves rolling in; for it was rather a wild night, and our small one-storeyed cottage stood by itself in a solitary part of the beach. How well I remember myself! sitting with the pen in my hand, uncertain how to begin; for I felt awkward, never having written to him since I was a child. At first I almost forgot what I had to write about. While musing I was startled by a noise like the opening of a window. Now, as I explained, our house was all on one flat, and we could easily step from any window to the beach. Shuddering with alarm, I hurried into Zillah's room. There, by the dim night-light, I saw her bed was empty. She had apparently dressed herself—for I saw none of her clothes—and crept out at the window. Terrified inexpressibly, I was about to follow her, when I saw the flutter of a shawl outside and heard her speaking.

"No, cousin—no, dear cousin! Don't ask me. I can't go away with you to-night. It would be very wrong when Miss Pryor knows nothing about it. If she had found us out, or threatened, and we were obliged to go——" (Immediately I saw that with a girl of Zillah's fierce obstinacy discovery would be most dangerous. I put out the light and kept quite still.)

"I can't, indeed I can't," pursued Zillah's voice, in answer to some urging which was inaudible; adding with a childish laugh: "You know, Cousin Augustus, it would never do for me to go and be married in a cotton dressing gown; and Miss Pryor keeps all my best clothes. Dear Miss Pryor! I would much rather have told her, only you say she would be so much the more surprised and pleased when I came back married. And you are quite sure that she shall always live with us, and never return to Yorkshire again!"

Her words, so childish, so unconscious of the wrong she was doing, perfectly startled me. All my notions of girlish devotion following its own wild will were put to flight. Here was a mere child led away by the dazzle of a new toy to the brink of a precipice. She evidently knew no more of love and marriage than a baby. For a little time longer the wicked—lover I cannot call him—suitor urged his suit, playing with her simplicity in a manner that he must have inwardly laughed at all the time. He lured her to matrimony by puerile pet names, such as "My angel"—by idle rhapsodies and pictures of fine houses and clothes. "I don't mind these things at all," said poor Zillah innocently; "only you say that when I am married I shall have nothing to do, and you will never scold me, and I shall have Miss Pryor always with me. Promise!" Here was a pause, until the child's simple voice was heard again: "I don't like that, cousin. I won't kiss you. Miss Pryor once said we ought never to kiss anybody unless we love them very much."

"And don't you love me, my adorable creature?"

"I—I'm not quite sure: sometimes I love you, and sometimes not; but I suppose I shall always when we are married."

"That must be very soon," said the lieutenant, and I thought I heard him trying to suppress a yawn. "Let us settle it at once, my dear, for it is late. If you will not come to-night, let me have the happiness, the entire felicity, of fetching you to-morrow."

"No, no," Zillah answered; "Miss Pryor will want me to help her to pack. We leave this day week; let me stay till the night before that; then come for me, and I'll have my best frock on, and we can be married in time to meet them all before the boat sails next day."

In any other circumstances I should have smiled at this child's idea of marriage, but now the crisis was far too real and awful; and the more her ignorance lightened her own error, the more it increased the crime of that bad man who was about to ruin her peace for ever. A little he tried to reverse her plan and make the marriage earlier; but Zillah was too steady. In the obstinacy of her character—in the little influence which, lover as he was, he seemed to have over her—I read her safeguard, past and present. It would just allow me time to save her in the only way she could be saved. I listened till I heard her say good-bye to her cousin, creep back into the dark room through the open window, and fasten it securely as before. Then I stole away to the parlour, and, supported by the strong excitement of the moment, wrote my letter to Mr. Sutherland. There would be in the six days just time for the arrival of an answer, or—himself. I left everything to him, merely stating the facts, knowing he would do right. At midnight I went to bed. Zillah was fast asleep. As I lay awake, hour after hour, I thanked Heaven that the poor child, deluded as she had been, knew nothing of what love was in its reality. She was at least spared that sorrow.

During all the week I contrived to keep Zillah as near me as was possible, consistent with the necessity of not awaking her suspicions. This was the more practicable, as she seemed to cling to me with an unwonted and even painful tenderness. The other girls grumbled sadly at our departure; but luckily all had been definitely arranged by their father, who had even, strange to say, given me money for the journey. He had likewise gracefully apologised for being obliged to let us travel alone, as he had himself some business engagements, while his son had lately rejoined his regiment. I really think the deceiving and deceived father fully credited the latter fact. Certainly they were a pretty pair! I made all my plans secure, and screwed up my courage as well as I could; but I own on the evening previous to our journey—the evening which, from several attesting proofs, I knew was still fixed for the elopement—I began to feel a good deal alarmed. Of Mr. Sutherland there were no tidings. At twilight I saw plainly that the sole hope must lie in my own presence of mind, my influence over Zillah, and my appeal to her sense of honour and affection.

I sent the children early to bed, saying I had letters to write, and prepared myself for whatever was to happen. Now many may think me foolish, and at times I thought myself so likewise, for not going at once to Zillah and telling her all I had discovered; but I knew her character better than that. The idea of being betrayed, waylaid, controlled, would drive her fierce Eastern nature into the very commission of the madness she contemplated. In everything I must trust to the impulse of the moment, and to the result of her suddenly discovering her own position and the villainous plans laid against her.

Never in my life do I remember a more anxious hour than that I spent sitting in the dark by the parlour window, whence, myself unseen, I could see all that passed without the house; for it was a lovely night: the moon high up over the loch and making visible the Antrim hills. I think in all moments of great peril one grows quiet; so did I. At eleven there was a sound of wheels on the beach, and the shadow of a man passed the window. I looked out. It was the most unromantic and commonplace elopement with an heiress; he was merely going to take her away on an outside car. There was no one with him but the carman, who was left whistling contentedly on the shore. The moment had come. With the energy of desperation, I put off the shawl in which I had wrapped myself in case I had to follow the child; for follow her I had determined to do were it necessary. Quietly, and with as ordinary a manner as I could assume, I walked into Zillah's room. She was just stepping from the window. She had on her best frock and shawl, poor innocent! with her favourite white bonnet, that I had lately trimmed for her, carefully tied up in a kerchief. I touched her shoulder.

"Zillah, where are you going?" She started and screamed. "Tell me; I must know," I repeated, holding her fast by the arm, while Augustus rather roughly pulled her by the other.

"Cousin, you hurt me!" she cried, and instinctively drew back. Then for the first time the lieutenant saw me.

I have often noticed that cunning and deceitful people—small villains, not great ones—are always cowards. Mr. Augustus drew back as if he had been shot. I took no notice of him, but still appealed to Zillah.

"Tell me, my child, the plain truth, as you always do; where were you going?"

She stammered out, "I was going to—to Belfast—to be married."

"To your cousin?"

She hung her head and murmured, "Yes."

At this frank confession the bridegroom interposed. He perhaps was the braver for reflecting that he had only women to deal with. He leapt in at the chamber window, and angrily asked me by what right I interfered. "I will tell you," said I, "if you have enough gentlemanly feeling to leave my apartment, and will speak with me in the open air." He retreated. I bolted the window, and, still keeping a firm hold of the trembling girl, met him outside the front door. It certainly was the oddest place for such a scene; but I did not wish to let him inside the house.

"Now, Miss Pryor," said he imperatively, but still politely—a Le Poer could not be otherwise—"will you be so kind as to let go that young lady, who has put herself under my protection, and intends honouring me with her hand?"

"Is that true, Zillah? Do you love this man, and voluntarily intend to marry him?"

"Yes, if you will let me, Miss Pryor. He told me you would be so pleased. He promised always to be kind to me, and never let me work. Please don't be angry with me, dear Miss Pryor. Oh, do let me marry my cousin!"

"Listen to me a few minutes, Zillah," said I, "and you shall choose." And then I told her, in as few words as I could, what her position was—how it had been concealed from her that she was an heiress, and how, by marrying her, her cousin Augustus would be master over all her wealth. So unworldly was she that I think the girl herself hardly understood me; but the lieutenant was furious.

"It is all a lie—an infamous cheat!" he cried. "Don't believe it, Zillah. Don't be frightened, little fool! I promised to marry you, and, by Heaven! marry you I will!"

"Lieutenant Le Poer," said I very quietly, "that may not be quite so easy as you think. However, *I* do not prevent you, as indeed I have no right; I only ask my dear child Zillah here to grant me one favour, as, for the sake of my love for her"—(here Zillah sobbed)—"I doubt not she will: that she should do as every other young woman of common-sense and delicacy would do, and wait until tomorrow, to ask the consent of one who will then probably be here, if he is not already arrived—her guardian, Mr. Andrew Sutherland."

Lieutenant Augustus burst out with an oath, probably mild in the mess-room, but very shocking here to two women's ears. Zillah crept farther from him and nearer to me.

"I'll not be cheated so!" stormed he. "Come, child, you'll trust your cousin? You'll come away to-night?" and he tried to lift her on the car, which had approached—the Irish driver evidently much enjoying the scene.

"No, cousin; not to-night," said the girl, resisting. "I'd rather wait and have Miss Pryor with me, and proper bridesmaids, and all that—that is, if I marry you at all, which I won't unless Miss Pryor thinks you will be kind to me. So good-bye till to-morrow, cousin." He was so enraged by this time that he tried forcibly to drag her on the car. But I wound my arms round my dear child's waist and shrieked for help.

"Faith, sir," said the sturdy Irishman, interfering half in amusement, half in indignation, "ye'd betther lave the women alone. I'd rayther not meddle with an abduction."

So Zillah was set free from the lieutenant's grasp, for, as I said before; a scoundrel is often a great coward. I drew the trembling and terrified girl into the house—he following with a storm of oaths and threatenings. At last I forcibly shut the door upon him and bolted him out. Whether this indignity was too much for the valorous soldier, or whether he felt sure that all chance was over, I know not; but when I looked out ten minutes after, the coast was clear. I took my erring, wronged, yet still more wronged than erring, child unto my bosom, and thanked Heaven that she was saved. The next morning Mr. Sutherland arrived.

After this night's events I have little to say, or else had rather say but little of what passed during the remainder of that summer. We all travelled to England together, going round by Yorkshire to leave Mr. Le Poer's daughters at their own home. This was Mr. Sutherland's plan, in order that the two girls should be kept in ignorance of the whole affair, and especially of their father's ill-deeds. What they suspected I know not; they were merely told that it was the desire of Zillah's guardian to take her and her governess home with him. So we parted at Halifax, and I never saw any of the family again. I had no scruples about thus quitting them, as I found out from Mr. Sutherland that I had been engaged solely as governess to his ward, and that he had himself paid my salary in advance, the whole of which, in some way or other, had been intercepted by Mr. Le Poer. The money, of course, was gone; but he had written to me with each remittance, and thus I had lost his letters. That was hard! I also found out, with great joy and comfort, that my Zillah was truly Zillah Le Poer—her father's legitimate heiress. All I had been led to believe was a cruel and wicked lie. The whole history of her father and mother was one of those family tragedies, only too frequent, which, the actors in them being dead, are best forgotten. I shall not revive the tale.

In late autumn Mr. Sutherland sailed for India. Before he quitted England he made me sole guardian in his stead over Zillah Le Poer, assigning for her a handsome maintenance. He said he hoped we should all live happily together—she, my mother, and I—until he came back. He spent a short time with us all at his country-seat—a time which, looking back upon, seems in its eight days like eight separate years.

I ought to speak of Zillah, the unmoved centre of so many convolving fates. She remained still and silent as ever—dull, grieved, humiliated. I told her gradually and gently the whole truth, and explained from how much she had been saved. She seemed grateful and penitent: her heart had never been touched by love; she was yet a mere child. The only evidence of womanly shame she gave was in keeping entirely out of her guardian's way. Nor did he take much notice of her except in reproaching himself to me with being neglectful of his charge; but he had so thoroughly trusted in the girl's uncle as being her best protector. The only remark he ever made on Zillah's personal self was, that she had beautiful eyes, adding, with a half-sigh, "that he liked dark Oriental eyes." One day his mother told me something which explained this. She said he had been engaged to a young lady in India, who on the eve of their marriage had died. He had never cared much for women's society since, and, his mother thought, would probably never marry. After his departure she told me the whole story. My heart bled over every pang that he had suffered: he was so good and noble a man. And when I knew about his indifference to all women, I felt the more gratefully what trust he showed in me by making me Zillah's guardian in his absence, and wishing me to write to him regularly of her welfare. The last words he said were to ask me to go and see his mother often; and then he bade God bless me, and called me "his dear friend." He was very kind always!

We had a quiet winter, for my health was not good—I being often delicate in winter-time. My mother and Zillah took care of me, and I was very grateful for their love. I got well at last, as the spring-time began, and went on in my old ways.

There are sometimes long pauses in one's life—deep rests or sleeps of years—in which month after month, and season after season, float on, each the same; during which the soul lies either quiet or torpid, as may be. Thus, without any trouble, joy, or change, we lived for several years—my mother, Zillah Le Poer, and I. One morning I found with a curious surprise, but without any of the horror which most women are supposed to feel at that fact, that I was thirty years old! We discovered by the same reckoning that Zillah was just nineteen. I remember she put her laughing face beside mine in the glass. There was a great difference, truly. I do not mean the difference in her from me, for I never compared that, but in her from her former self. She had grown up into a woman, and, as the glass told her, and my own eyes told me, a very striking woman too. I was little of a judge of beauty myself; still, I knew well that everybody we met thought her handsome. Likewise, she had grown up beautiful in mind as well as in body. I was very proud of my dear child. I well remember this day, when she was nineteen and I thirty. I remember it, I say, because our kind friend in India had remembered it likewise, and sent us each a magnificent shawl; far too magnificent it was for a little body like me, but it became Zillah splendidly. She tucked me under her arm as if I had been a little girl, and walked me up and down the room; for she was of a cheerful, gay temper now—just the one to make an old heart young again, to flash upon a worn spirit with the brightness of its own long-past morning. I recollect thinking this at the time—I wish I had thought so oftener! But it matters little: I only chronicle this day, as being the first when Zillah unconsciously put herself on a level with me, becoming thenceforward my equal—no longer a mere pet and a child.

About this time—I may as well just state the fact to comfort other maidens of thirty years' standing—I received an offer of marriage, the first I ever had. He who asked me was a gentleman of my own age, an old acquaintance, though never a very intimate friend. I examined myself well, with great humility and regret, for he was an excellent man; but I found I could not marry him. It was very strange that he should ask me, I thought. My mother, proud and pleased—first, because I had had the honour of a proposal; secondly, that it was refused, and she kept her child still—would have it that the circumstance was not strange at all. She said many women were handsomer and more attractive at thirty than they had ever been in their lives. My poor, fond, deluded and deluding mother, in whose sight even I was fair! That night I was foolish enough to look long into the glass, at my quiet little face and my pale, gray-blue eyes—not dark, like Zillah's—foolish enough to count narrowly the white threads that were coming one by one into my hair. This trouble—I mean the offer of marriage—I did not quite get over for many weeks, even months.

The following year of my life there befell me a great pang. Of this—a grief never to be forgotten, a loss never to be restored—I cannot even now say more than is implied in three words—*my mother died!* After that Zillah and I lived together alone for twelve months or more.

There are some scenes in our life—landscape scenes, I mean—that we remember very clearly: one strikes me now. A quiet, soft May-day; the hedges just in their first green, the horse-chestnuts white with flowers; the long, silent country-lanes swept through by a travelling-carriage, in the which two women, equally silent, sat—Zillah Le Poer and I. It was the month before her coming of age, and she was going to meet her guardian, who had just returned from India. Mrs. Sutherland had received a letter from Southampton, and immediately sent for us into the country to meet her son, her "beloved Andrew." I merely repeat the words as I remember Zillah's doing so, and laughing at the ugly name. I never thought it ugly. When we had really started, however, Zillah ceased laughing, and became grave, probably at the recollection of that humiliating circumstance which first brought her acquainted with her guardian. But, despite this ill-omened beginning, her youth had blossomed into great perfection. As she sat there before me, fair in person, well-cultured in mind, and pure and virgin in heart—for I had so kept her out of harm's way that, though nearly twenty-one, I knew she had never been "in love" with any man—as she sat thus, I felt proud and glad of her, feeling sure that Mr. Sutherland would say I had well fulfilled the charge he gave.

We drove to the lodge-gates. An English country-house is always fair to see: this was very beautiful. I remembered it seven years ago; only then it was autumn, and now spring. Zillah remembered it likewise; she drew back, and I heard her whisper uneasily, "Now we shall soon see Mr. Sutherland." I did not answer her a word. We rolled up the avenue under the large chestnut-trees. I saw some one standing at the portico; then I think the motion of the carriage must have made me dizzy, for all grew indistinct, except a firm, kind hand holding me as I stepped down, and the words, "Take care, my dear Cassia!" It was Mr. Sutherland! He scarcely observed Zillah, till in the hall I introduced her to him. He seemed surprised, startled, pleased. Talking of her to me that evening, he said he had not thought she would have grown up thus; and I noticed him look at her at times with a pensive kindness. Mrs. Sutherland whispered to me that the lady he had been engaged to was a half-caste like Zillah, which accounted for it. His mother had been right: he had come back as he went out—unmarried.

When Zillah went to bed she was full of admiration for her guardian. He was so tall, so stately. Then his thick, curling, fair hair—just like a young man's, with scarcely a shadow of gray. She would not believe that he was over forty—ten years older than myself—until by some pertinacity I had impressed this fact upon her. And then she said it did not signify, as she liked such "dear old souls" as he and I much better than any young people. Her fervour of admiration made me smile; but after this night I observed that the expression of it gradually ceased. Though I was not so demonstrative as Zillah, it will not be supposed but that I was truly glad to see my old friend Mr. Sutherland. He was very kind, talked to me long of past things, and as he cast a glance on my black dress I saw his lips quiver; he took my hand and pressed it like a brother. God bless him for that! But one thing struck me—a thing I had not calculated on—the alteration seven years had made in us both. When he took me down to dinner I accidentally caught sight of our two figures in the large pier-glass.[1] Age tells so differently on man and woman: I remembered the time when he was a grown man and I a mere girl; now he looked a stately gentleman in the prime of life, and I a middle-aged, old-maidish woman. Perhaps something more than years had done this; yet it was quite natural, only I had never thought of it before. So, when that first meeting was over, with the excitement, pleasurable or otherwise, that it brought as a matter of course to us all—when we had severally bade each other good-night, and Mr. Sutherland had said, smiling, that he was glad it was only good-night, not good-bye—when the whole house was quiet and asleep, I, to use the Psalmist's solemn words: "*At night on my bed I communed with my own heart in my chamber, and was still.*"[2]

"Cassia, I want to speak to you particularly," said Mr. Sutherland to me one morning as, after breakfast, he was about to go into his study. Zillah placed herself in the doorway with the pretty obstinacy, half-womanish, half-girlish, that she sometimes used with her guardian—much to my surprise. Zillah was on excellent terms with him, considering their brief acquaintance of three weeks. In that time she had treated him as I in my whole lifetime had never ventured to do—wilfully, jestingly, even crossly; yet he seemed to like it. They were very social and merry, for his disposition had apparently grown more cheerful as he advanced in life. Their relation was scarcely like guardian and ward, but that of

---

1 Mirror.

2 From Psalm 77:6.

perfect equality—pleasant and confidential, which somewhat surprised me, until I recollected what opportunities they had of intercourse, and what strong friendships are sometimes formed even in a single week or fortnight when people are shut up together in a rather lonely country-house. This was the state of things among us all on the morning when Mr. Sutherland called me to his study. Zillah wanted to go likewise. "Not to-day," he answered her, very gently and smilingly; "I have business to talk over with Miss Pryor." (I knew he said "Miss Pryor" out of respect, yet it hurt me—I had been "Cassia" with him so many years. Perhaps he thought I was outgrowing my baby-name now.)

The business he wished to speak of was about Zillah's coming of age next week, and what was to be done on the occasion. "Should he, ought he, to give a ball, a dinner, anything of that sort? Would Zillah like it?"

This was a great concession, for in old times he always disliked society. I answered that I did not think such display necessary, but I would try to find out Zillah's mind. I did so. It was an innocent, girlish mind, keenly alive to pleasure and new to everything. The consequences were natural—the ball must be. A little she hesitated when I hinted at her guardian's peculiarities, and offered cheerfully to renounce her delight. But he, his eyes beaming with a deeper delight still, would not consent. So the thing was settled. It was a very brilliant affair, for Mr. Sutherland spared no expense. He seemed to take a restless eagerness in providing for his young favourite everything she could desire. Nay, in answer to her wayward entreaties, he even consented to open the ball with her, though saying "he was sure he would make an old idiot of himself." That was not likely! I watched them walk down the room together, and heard many people say, with a smile, what a handsome pair they were, notwithstanding the considerable difference of age. It was a very quiet evening to me. Being strange to almost every one there, I sat near old Mrs. Sutherland in a corner. Mr. Sutherland asked me to dance once, but I did not feel strong, and indeed for the last few years I had almost given up dancing. He laughed, and said merrily, "It was not fair for him to be beginning life just when I ended it." A true word spoken in jest. But I only smiled.

The ball produced results not unlikely, when it was meant for the introduction into society of a young woman, handsome, attractive, and an heiress. A week or two after Zillah's birthday Mr. Sutherland called me once more into his study. I noticed he looked rather paler and less composed than usual. He forgot even to ask me to sit down, and we stood together by the fireplace, which I remember was filled with a great vase of lilacs that Zillah had insisted on placing there. It filled the room with a strong, rich scent, which now I never perceive without its calling back to mind that room and that day. He said, "I have had a letter to-day on which I wish to consult with you before showing it to Miss Le Poer." I was rather startled by the formal word, since he usually said "Zillah," as was natural. "It is a letter—scarcely surprising—in fact to be expected after what I noticed at the dinner-party yesterday; in fact—— But you had better read it yourself." He took the letter from his desk and gave it to me. It was an earnest and apparently sincere application for the hand of his ward. The suitor was of good family and moderate prospects. I had noticed he was very attentive to Zillah at the ball, and on some occasions since; still, I was a good deal surprised, more so even than Mr. Sutherland, who had evidently watched her closer than I. I gave him back the letter in silence, and avoided looking at his face.

"Well, Cassia," he said after a pause, and with an appearance of gaiety, "what is to be done? You women are the best counsellors in these matters." I smiled, but both he and I very soon became grave once more. "It is a thing to be expected," continued he in a voice rather formal and hard. "With Zillah's personal attractions and fortune she was sure to receive many offers. Still, it is early to begin these affairs." I reminded him that she was twenty-one. "True, true. She might, under other circumstances, have been married long before this. Do you think that she——" I suppose he was going to ask me whether she was likely to accept Mr. French, or whether she had hitherto formed any attachment. But probably delicacy withheld him, for he suddenly stopped and omitted the question. Soon he went on in the same steady tone: "I think Zillah ought to be made acquainted with this circumstance. Mr. French states that this letter to me is the first confession of his feelings. That was honourable on his part. He is a gentleman of good standing, though far her inferior in fortune. People might say that he wanted her property to patch up the decayed estate at Weston-Brook." This was spoken bitterly, very bitterly for a man of such kind nature as Andrew Sutherland. He seemed conscious of it, and added: "I may wrong him, and if so I regret it. But do you not think, Cassia, that of all things it must be most despicable, most mean, most galling to a man of any pride or honest feeling, the thought of the world's saying that he married his wife for money, as a prop to his falling fortunes, or a shield to his falling honour? I would die a thousand deaths first!"

In the passion of the moment the red colour rushed violently to his cheek, and then he became more pallid than ever. I beheld him: my eyes were opened now. I held fast by the marble chimney-piece, so that I could stand quite upright, firm, and quiet. He walked hurriedly to the window and flung it open, saying the scent of the lilacs was too strong. When he came back we were both ready to talk again. I believe I spoke first—to save him the pain of doing so. "I have no idea," said I, and I said truly, "what answer Zillah will give to this letter. Hitherto I have known all her feelings, and am confident that while she stayed with me her heart was untouched." Here I waited for him to speak, but he did not. I went on: "Mr. French is very agreeable, and she seems to like him; but a girl's heart, if of any value at all, is rarely won in three meetings. I think, however, that Zillah ought to be made acquainted with this letter. Will you tell her, or shall I?"

"Go you and do it—a woman can best deal with a woman in these cases. And," he added, rising slowly and looking down upon me from his majestic height with that grave and self-possessed smile which was likewise as sweet as any woman's, "tell Zillah from me, that though I wish her to marry in her own rank and with near quality of fortune, to save her from all those dangers of mercenary offers to which an heiress is so cruelly exposed, still, both now and at all times, I leave her to the dictates of her own affections, and her happiness will ever be my chief consideration in life." He spoke with formal serenity until the latter words, when his voice sank a little. Then he led me to the door, and I went out.

Zillah lay on a sofa reading a love-story. Her crisped black hair was tossed about the crimson cushions, and her whole figure was that of rich Eastern luxuriance. She had always rather a fantastic way of dress, and now she looked almost like a princess out of the *Arabian Nights*.[1] Even though her skin was that of a half-caste, and her little hands were not white but brown, there was no denying that she was a very beautiful woman. I felt it—saw it—knew it! After a minute's pause I went to her side; she jumped up and kissed me, as she was rather fond of doing. Her kisses were

---

1 *The Thousand and One Nights*, a collection of Middle Eastern and Indian stories dating back to the Islamic Golden Age (c. ninth–thirteenth centuries). In the frame story, the young sultana Scheherazade relates stories about such characters as Aladdin, Ali Baba, and Sinbad to her jealous husband, the sultan Shahryar, in the hopes of saving herself from execution by keeping him entertained.

very strange to me just then. I came as quickly as possible to my errand, and gave her the letter to read. As she glanced through it her cheeks flushed and her lips began to curl. She threw the letter on my lap, and said abruptly, "Well, and what of that?" I began a few necessary explanations. Zillah stopped me.

"Oh, I heard something of the sort from Mr. French last night. I did not believe him, nor do I now. He is only making a jest of me."

I answered that this was impossible. In my own mind I was surprised at Zillah's having known the matter before, and having kept it so quiet. Mr. French's statement about his honourable reticence towards the lady of his devotions must have been untrue. Still, this was not so remarkable as Zillah's own secrecy on the subject. "Why did you not tell me, my dear?" said I. "You know your happiness is of the first importance to me as well as to your guardian." And, rather hesitatingly, I repeated word for word, as near as I could, Mr. Sutherland's message. Zillah half hid her face within the cushions, and then drew it out burning red.

"He thinks I am going to accept the creature, then? He would have me marry a conceited, chattering, mean-looking, foolish boy!" (Now Mr. French was certainly twenty-five.) "One, too, that only wants me for my fortune, and nothing else. It is very wrong and cruel and unkind of him, and you may go and tell him so."

"Tell whom?" said I, bewildered by this outburst of indignation and great confusion of personal pronouns.

"Mr. Sutherland, of course! Whom else would I tell? Whose opinion else do I care for? Go and say to him—— No," she added abruptly, "no, you needn't trouble him with anything about such a foolish girl as I. Just say I shall not marry Mr. French, and will he be so kind as to give him his answer, and bid him let me alone?" Here, quite exhausted with her wrath, Zillah sank back and took to her book, turning her head from me. But I saw that she did not read one line, that her motionless eyes were fixed and full of a strange deep expression. I began to cease wondering what the future would bring. Very soon afterwards I went back to Mr. Sutherland, and told him all that had passed, just the plain facts without any comments of my own. He apparently required none. I found him sitting composedly with some papers before him—he had for the last few days been immersed in business which seemed rather to trouble him. He started a little as I entered, but immediately came forward and listened with a quiet aspect to the message I had to bring. I could not tell whether it made him happy or the contrary; his countenance could be at times so totally impassive that no friend, dearest or nearest, could ever find out from it anything he did not wish to betray.

"The matter is settled, then," said he gravely; "I will write to Mr. French today, and perhaps it would be as well if we never alluded to what has passed. I, at least, shall not do it; tell Zillah so. But, in the future, say I entreat that she will keep no secret back from you. Remember this, my dear Cassia: watch over her as you love her—and you do love her?" continued he, grasping my hand. I answered that I did, and, God knows, even then I told no lie. She was a very dear child to me always! Mr. Sutherland seemed quite satisfied and at rest. He bade me a cheerful good-bye, which I knew meant that I should go away, so accordingly I went. Passing the drawing-room door, I saw Zillah lying in her old position on the sofa; so I would not disturb her, but went and walked for an hour under a clump of fir-trees in the garden. They made a shadow dark and grave and still; it was pleasanter than being on the lawn, among the flowers, the sunshine, and the bees. I did not come in until dinner-time. There were only ourselves, just a family party—Mr. Sutherland did not join us until we reached the dining-room door. I noticed that Zillah's colour changed as he approached, and that all dinner-time she hardly spoke to him; but he behaved to her as usual. He was rather thoughtful, for, as he told me privately, he had some trifling business anxieties burdening him just then; otherwise he seemed the same. Nevertheless, whether it was his fault or Zillah's, in a few days the fact grew apparent to me that they were not such good friends as heretofore. A restraint, a discomfort, a shadow scarcely tangible, yet still there, was felt between them. Such a cloud often rises—a mist that comes just before the day-dawn; or, as happens sometimes, before the night.

For many days—how many I do not recollect, since about this time all in the house and in the world without seemed to go on so strangely—for many days afterwards nothing happened of any consequence, except that one Sunday afternoon I made a faint struggle of politeness in some remark about "going home" and "encroaching on their hospitality," which was met with such evident pain and alarm by all parties that I was silent; so we stayed yet longer. One morning—it was high summer now—we were sitting at breakfast: we three only, as Mrs. Sutherland never rose early. I was making tea, Zillah near me, and Mr. Sutherland at the foot of the table. He looked anxious, and did not talk much, though I remember he rose up once to throw a handful of crumbs to a half-tame thrush who had built on the lawn—he was always so kind to every living thing. "There, my fine bird, take some home to your wife and weans[1]!" said he pleasantly; but at the words became grave, even sad, once more. He had his letters beside him, and opened them successively until he came to *one*—a momentous one, I knew; for, though he never moved, but read quietly on, every ray of colour went out of his face. He dropped his head upon his hand, and sat so long in that attitude that we were both frightened.

"Is anything the matter?" I said gently, for Zillah was dumb.

"Did you speak?" he answered, with a bewildered stare. "Forgive me; I—I have had bad news"—and he tried to resume the duties of the meal, but it was impossible; he was evidently crushed, as even the strongest and bravest men will be, for the moment, under some great and unexpected shock. We said to him—I repeat *we*, because, though Zillah spoke not, her look was enough, had he seen it—we said to him those few soothing things that women can, and ought to, say in such a time. "Ay," he answered quite unmanned—"ay, you are very kind. I think—if I could speak to some one—Cassia, will you come?" He rose slowly, and held out his hand to me. *To me!* That proof of his confidence, his tenderness, his friendship, I have always remembered, and thought, with thankful heart, that though not made to give him happiness, I have sometimes done him a little good when he was in trouble.

We walked together from the room. I heard a low sob behind us, but had no power to stay. Besides, a momentary pang mattered little; the sobs would be hushed ere long. Standing behind the chair where he sat, I heard the story of Mr. Sutherland's misfortunes—misfortunes neither strange nor rare in the mercantile world. In one brief word, he was ruined; that is, so far as a man can be considered ruined who has enough left to pay all his creditors and start in the world afresh as a penniless honest man. He told me this—an every-day story; nay, it had been my own father's—told it me with great composure, and I listened with the same. I was acquainted with all these kind of business matters of old. It was very strange, but I felt no grief, no pity for his losses; I only felt, on my own account, a burning, avaricious thirst for gold; a frantic envy—a mad longing to have for a single day, a single hour, wealth in millions.

"Yes, it must be so," said he, when, after talking to me a little more, I saw the hard muscles of his face relax, and he grew patient, ready to bear his troubles like a man—like Andrew

1 Offspring or children, deriving from the Scottish for "little ones."

Sutherland. "Yes, I must give up this house, and all my pleasant life here; but I can do it, since I shall be alone." And then he added in a low tone: "I am glad, Cassia, very glad of two things: my mother's safe settlement, and the winding-up last month of all my affairs with—Miss Le Poer."

"When," said I, after a pause—"when do you intend to tell Zillah what has happened?" I felt feverishly anxious that she should know all, and that I should learn how she would act.

"Tell Zillah? Ay," he repeated, "tell her at once—tell her at once." And then he sank back into his chair, muttering something about "its signifying little now."

I left him, and, with my heart nerved as it were to anything, went back to the room where Zillah was. Her eyes met me with a bitter, fierce, jealous look—jealous of me, foolish child!—until I told her what had happened to our friend. Then she wept, but only for a moment, until a light broke upon her. "What does it signify?" cried she, echoing, curiously enough, his own words. "I am of age—I can do just what I like; so I will give my guardian all my money. Go back and tell him so!" I hesitated. "I tell you I will: all I have in the world is not too good for him. Everything belonging to me is his, and——" Here she stopped, and, catching my fixed look, became covered with confusion. Still, the generous heart did not waver. "And, when he has my fortune, you and I will go and live together, and be governesses." I felt the girl was in earnest, that she did not wish to deceive me; and though I let her deceive herself a little longer, it was with joy—ay, with joy, that in the heart I clasped to mine was such unselfishness, such true nobility, not unworthy even of what it was about to win. I went once more through the hall—the long, cool, silent hall, which I trod so dizzily, daring not to pause—unto Mr. Sutherland's presence. "Well!" he said, looking up.

I told—in what words I cannot remember now, but solemnly, faithfully, as if I were answering my account before Heaven—the truth, and the whole truth. He listened, pressing his hands on his eyes, and then gave vent to one heavy sigh like a woman's sob. At last he rose and walked feebly to the door. There he paused, as though to account for his going. "I ought to thank her, you know. It must not be—not by any means. Still, I ought to go and thank her—the—dear—child!" His voice ceased, broken by emotion. Once more he held out his hand. I grasped it and said, "Go!" At the parlour door he stopped, apparently for me to precede him in entering there; but, as if accidentally, I passed on and let him enter alone. Whether he knew it or not, I knew clear as light what would happen then and there. The door shut—they two being within, and I without. In an hour I came back towards the house. I had been wandering somewhere, I think, under the fir-wood. It was broad noon, but I felt very cold; it was always cold under those trees. I had no way to pass but near the parlour window, and some insane attraction made me look up as I went by. They were standing—they two—close together, as lovers stand. His arm folded her close; his face, all radiant, yet trembling with tenderness, was pressed upon hers—O my God!

I am half inclined to blot out the last sentence, as it seems so foolish to dilate on the love-makings of people now twelve years married; and besides, growing older, one feels the more how rarely and how solemnly the Holy Name ought to be mingled with any mere burst of human emotion. But I think the All-Merciful One would pardon it then. Of course no reader will marvel at my showing emotion over the union of these my two dearest objects on earth.

From that union I can now truly say I have derived the greatest comforts of my life. They were married quickly, as I urged, Mr. Sutherland settling his wife's whole property upon herself. This was the only balm his manly pride could know; and no greater proof could he give of his passionate love for her than that he humbled himself to marry an heiress. As to what the world thought, no one could ever suspect the shadow of mercenary feeling in Andrew Sutherland. All was as it should be—and so best.

After Zillah's marriage I took a situation abroad. Mr. Sutherland was very angry when he knew; but I told them I longed for the soft Italian air, and could not live an idle life on any account. So they let me go, knowing, as he smilingly said, "that Cassia could be obstinate when she had a mind—that her will, like her heart, was as firm as a rock." Ah me!

When I came back, it was to a calm, contented, and cheerful middle-age; to the home of a dear brother and sister; to the love of a new generation; to a life filled with peace of heart and thankfulness towards God; to——

Hey-day! writing at this moment becomes quite impossible; for there peeps a face in at my bedroom door, and while I live, not for worlds shall my young folk know that Aunt Cassie is an authoress.[1] Therefore, good-bye, pen!—And now come in, my namesake, my darling, my fair-haired Cassia, with her mother's smile, and her father's eyes and brow—I may kiss both now. Ah, God in heaven bless thee, my dear, dear child!

---

1 The 1851, 1853, and 1859 texts have "Aunt Cassia" for "Aunt Cassie."

Appendix A: Dinah Mulock Craik on Gender Issues and Female Employment

[Throughout the nineteenth century, women's educational opportunities—and therefore their ability to seek gratifying, independent, and self-sustaining lives within society—were slow to advance with the times. In *A Woman's Thoughts about Women* (1858), which originally appeared in *Chambers's Edinburgh Journal* in 1857, Craik stressed that Victorian daughters should be educated toward independence and self-reliance. She also entered the debate over the governess profession in *A Woman's Thoughts*, where she advocated for stricter educational standards for governesses as a means of decreasing the number of unqualified women who seek employment as teachers (see Appendix A1). Toward the end of her life, Craik returned to the topic of women's education and employment in "Concerning Men, By a Woman," published in the October 1887 issue of *Cornhill.* In that essay, Craik gave voice to women's discontent by advocating for increased educational and career options for them. She examined the ways in which the men and women of her society failed to fully understand and respect one another and, in so doing, continually kept one another from reaching their respective full potentials, both at home and in the workplace (see A2).]

1. From Dinah Mulock Craik, *A Woman's Thoughts about Women* (London: Hurst and Blackett, 1858), 24–26, 34–36, 43–49

From Chapter 2, "Self-Dependence"

Were it our ordinary lot, were every woman living to have either father, brother, or husband, to watch over and protect her, then, indeed, the harsh but salutary doctrine of self-dependence need never be heard of. But it is not so. In spite of the pretty ideals of poets, the easy taken-for-granted truths of old-fashioned educators of female youth, this fact remains patent to any person of common sense and experience, that in the present day, whether voluntarily or not, one-half of our women are *obliged* to take care of themselves—obliged to look solely to themselves for maintenance, position, occupation, amusement, reputation, life.

Of course I refer to the large class for which these Thoughts are meant—the single women; who, while most needing the exercise of self-dependence, are usually the very last in whom it is inculcated, or even permitted. From babyhood they are given to understand that helplessness is feminine and beautiful; helpfulness,—except in certain received forms of manifestation—unwomanly and ugly. The boys may do a thousand things which are "not proper for little girls."

And herein, I think, lies the great mistake at the root of most women's education, that the law of their existence is held to be, not Right, but Propriety; a certain received notion of womanhood, which has descended from certain excellent great-grandmothers, admirably suited for some sorts of their descendants, but totally ignoring the fact that each sex is composed of individuals, differing in character almost as much from one another as from the opposite sex. For do we not continually find womanish men and masculine women? and some of the finest types of character we have known among both sexes, are they not often those who combine the qualities of both? Therefore, there must be somewhere a standard of abstract right, including manhood and womanhood, and yet superior to either. One of the first of its common laws, or common duties, is this of self-dependence.

[...]

We *must* help ourselves. In this curious phase of social history, when marriage is apparently ceasing to become the common lot, and a happy marriage the most uncommon lot of all, we must educate our maidens into what is far better than any blind clamour for ill-defined "rights"—into what ought always to be the foundation of rights—duties. And there is one, the silent practice of which will secure to them almost every right they can fairly need—the duty of self-dependence. Not after any Amazonian fashion; no mutilating of fair womanhood in order to assume the unnatural armour of men; but simply by the full exercise of every faculty, physical, moral, and intellectual, with which Heaven has endowed us all, severally and collectively, in different degrees; allowing no one to rust or lie idle, merely because their owner is a woman. And, above all, let us lay the foundation of all real womanliness by teaching our girls from their cradle that the priceless pearl of decorous beauty, chastity of mind as well as body, exists in themselves alone; that a single-hearted and pure-minded woman may go through the world, like Spenser's Una,[1] suffering, indeed, but never defenceless; foot-sore and smirched, but never tainted; exposed, doubtless, to many trials, yet never either degraded or humiliated, unless by her own act she humiliates herself.

1 A virtuous character in Edmund Spenser's (1552–99) *The Faerie Queene* (1590) who represents truth, wholeness, and the Protestant faith.

For heaven's sake—for the sake of "womanhede," the most heavenly thing next angelhood, (as men tell us when they are courting us, and which it depends upon ourselves to make them believe in all their lives)—young girls, trust yourselves; rely on yourselves! Be assured that no outward circumstances will harm you while you keep the jewel of purity in your bosom, and are ever ready with the steadfast, clean right hand, of which, till you use it, you never know the strength, though it be only a woman's hand.

From Chapter 3, "Female Professions"

If, in the most solemn sense, not one woman in five thousand is fit to be a mother, we may safely say that not two out of that number are fit to be governesses. Consider all that the office implies: very many of a mother's duties, with the addition of considerable mental attainments, firmness of character, good sense, good temper, good breeding; patience, gentleness, loving-kindness. In short, every quality that goes to make a perfect woman, is required of her who presumes to undertake the education of one single little child.

Does any one pause to reflect what a "little child" is? Not sentimentally, as a creature to be philosophised upon, painted and poetised; nor selfishly, as a kissable, scoldable, sugar-plum-feedable plaything; but as a human soul and body, to be moulded, instructed, and influenced, in order that it in its turn may mould, instruct, and influence unborn generations. And yet, in face of this awful responsibility, wherein each deed and word of hers may bear fruit, good or ill, to indefinite ages, does nearly every educated gentlewoman thrown upon her own resources, nearly every half-educated "young person" who wishes by that means to step out of her own sphere into the one above it, enter upon the vocation of a governess.

Whether it really is her vocation, she never stops to think; and yet, perhaps, in no calling is a personal bias more indispensable. For knowledge, and the power of imparting it intelligibly, are two distinct and often opposite qualities; the best student by no means necessarily makes the best teacher: nay, when both faculties are combined, they are sometimes neutralised by some fault of disposition, such as want of temper or of will. And allowing all these, granting every possible intellectual and practical competency, there remains still doubtful the moral influence, which, according to the source from which it springs, may ennoble or corrupt a child for life.

All these are facts so trite and so patent, that one would almost feel it superfluous to state them, did we not see how utterly they are ignored day by day by even sensible people; how parents go on lavishing expense on their house, dress, and entertainments—everything but the education of their children; sending their boys to cheap boarding-schools, and engaging for their daughters governesses at 20*l.* a year, or daily tuition at sixpence an hour; and how, as a natural result, thousands of incapable girls, and ill-informed, unscrupulous women, go on professing to teach everything under the sun, adding lie upon lie, and meanness upon meanness—often through no voluntary wickedness, but sheer helplessness, because they must either do that or starve!

Yet, all the while we expect our rising generation to turn out perfection; instead of which we find it—what?

I do solemnly aver, having seen more than one generation of young girls grow up into womanhood—that the fairest and best specimens of our sex that I have ever known have been among those who have never gone to school, or scarcely ever had a regular governess.

Surely such a fact as this—I put it to general experience, whether it is not a fact?—indicates some great flaw in the carrying out of this large branch of women's work. How is it to be remedied? I believe, like all reformations, it must begin at the root—with the governesses themselves.

Unless a woman has a decided pleasure and facility in teaching, an honest knowledge of everything she professes to impart, a liking for children, and above all, a strong moral sense of her responsibility towards them, for her to attempt to enrol herself in the scholastic order is absolute profanation. Better turn shopwoman, needlewoman, lady's-maid—even become a decent housemaid, and learn how to sweep a floor, than belie her own soul, and peril many other souls, by entering upon what is, or ought to be, a female "ministry," unconsecrated for, and incapable of the work.

"But," say they, "work we must have. Competition is so great, that if we did not profess to do everything, it would be supposed we could do nothing: and so we should starve."

Yet, what is competition? A number of people attempting to do what most of them can only half do, and some cannot do at all—thereby "cutting one another's throats," as the saying is, so long as their incapacity is concealed; when it is found out, starving. There may be exceptions from exceeding misfortune and the like—but in the long run, I believe it will be found that few women, really competent to what they undertake, be it small or great, starve for want of work to do. So, in this case, no influence is so deeply felt in a house, or so anxiously retained, if only from self-interest, as the influence of a good governess over the children; among the innumerable throng of teachers, there is nothing more difficult to find—or more valuable when found, to judge by the high terms asked and obtained by many professors—than a lady who can teach only a single thing, solidly, conscientiously, and well.

In this, as in most social questions, where to theorise is easy and to practise very difficult, it will often be found that the silent undermining of an evil is safer than the loud outcry against it. If every governess, so far as her power extends, would strive to elevate the character of her profession by elevating its members, many of the unquestionable wrongs and miseries of governess-ship would gradually right themselves. A higher standard of capability would weed out much cumbersome mediocrity; and, competition lessened, the value of labour would rise. I say "the value of labour," because, when we women do work, we must learn to rate ourselves at no ideal and picturesque value, but simply as *labourers*—fair and honest competitors in the field of the world; and our wares as mere merchandise, where money's worth alone brings money, or has any right to expect it.

2. From Dinah Mulock Craik, "Concerning Men, By a Woman," *Cornhill* (October 1887): 371–73, 376–77

Loving and serving is a woman's destiny, but it should be done in a right way. To yield to a man when you know he is in the wrong, to teach others that he must be yielded to whether right or wrong, is to place him on a pedestal where not one man in twenty thousand could stand steady. The unspoken creed of many a household, especially in the last generation, that the girls must always give in to the boys, that endless money should be spent on the boys' education and career in the world, while the girls must shift for themselves—this it is, I believe, which has brought about that painful reaction, in which women are gradually unsexing themselves, trying to do a multitude of things which Nature never meant them to do, and losing sight of that which she did mean, viz. that they should be, first the wives and mothers, and, failing that, the friends, consolers, and helpers of men.

This they can be in a hundred ways, without attempting the impossible, and without controverting the supposed Christian doctrine that the man is the head of the woman; as he ought to be if he deserves it, but which when truly deserving he will seldom obnoxiously claim to be. It is a curious fact, which I have noticed throughout my life, that the strongest, noblest, wisest men are those who are the least afraid of granting to women all the "rights" they could possibly desire, and the most generous in allowing them all the qualities, so often dormant through neglected education, which they possess in common with men.

One of these, strange as it may appear, is the "business faculty," usually attributed to men only—except in France, where, especially among the *bourgeoisie*, "Madame" does the business of the family, which prospers accordingly. Despite her revolutions there is no richer, more economical, nor more thriving country than France, and none where women do more work or are more highly regarded.

"I would never let my daughter marry an Englishman," said to me once a French lady, a better "business woman" and doing daily more practical work than most men; "vos maris Anglais sont toujours tyrans." I hope not! but I think English husbands and fathers would be wiser if, instead of saying contemptuously that "women never understand business," they taught their womenkind to understand it. This would lighten their own hands amazingly, take from them half the worries which convert them into supposed "tyrants," besides being an incalculable advantage to the women themselves.

Men, from their large *ego*, have a tendency to take interest chiefly in their own affairs, to see things solely from their own point of view, and to judge things, not as they are, but as the world will look at them with reference to their individual selves. But their power and inclination to take trouble are rarely equal to a woman's. Her very narrowness makes her more conscientious and reliable in matters of minute detail. A man's horizon is wider, his vision larger, his physical and intellectual strength generally greater than a woman's; but he is as a rule less prudent, less careful, less able to throw himself out of himself, and into the interests of other people. Granted a capable woman, and one who has had even a tithe of the practical education that all men have or are supposed to have, she will do a matter of business, say an executorship, secretaryship, &c., as well as any man, or even better than most men, because she will take more pains.

Did girls get from childhood the same business training as boys, and were it clearly understood in all families that it is no credit but rather a discredit for women to hang helpless on the men instead of doing their own work, and if necessary earning their own living, I believe society would be not the worse but the better for the change. Men would find out that the more they elevate women the greater use they get out of them. If instead of a man working himself to death for his unmarried daughters, and then leaving them ignominiously dependent upon male relations, he educated them to independence, made them able both to maintain and to protect themselves, it would save him and them a world of unhappiness. They would cease to be either the rivals—a very hopeless rivalry—or the playthings first and afterwards the slaves of men; and become, as was originally intended, their co-mates, equal and yet different, each sex supplying the other's deficiencies, and therefore fitted to work together, not apart, for the good of the world.

[...]

The relation between men and women ought to be as equal and as righteous as their love; also as clear-sighted, that by means of it each may educate and elevate the other; both looking beyond each other to that absolute right and perfect love, without which all human love must surely soon or late melt away in disenchantment, distaste, or even actual dislike. For love can die—there is no truth more certain and more terrible; and each human being that lives carries within himself or herself the possibility of being its murderer.

It will be seen that in all my judgments I have held a medium course, because, to me at least, this appears the only one possible. Neither sex can benefit by over-exalting or lowering the other. They are meant to work together, side by side, for mutual help and comfort, each tacitly supplying the other's deficiencies, without recriminations, or discussions as to what qualities are or are not possessed by either. The instant they begin to fight about their separate rights they are almost sure to forget their mutual duties, which are much more important to the conservation of society.

Appendix B: The British Empire, Race, and the "Eurasian Question"

[The excerpts below highlight the prevailing attitudes toward the mixed-race "Eurasian" community in India during the nineteenth century. This ethnic group was the subject of numerous British government reports that attempted to describe the group's population and classify its status within the wider Anglo-Indian community (see Appendix B1). Some sympathetic accounts of Eurasians appeared, but the majority of descriptions (written primarily by the British resident in India) tended to be uninformed and prejudiced against the community. The various contemporary attitudes toward Eurasians are represented in A.D. Rowe's portrait of the group in *Every-day Life in India* (B2) and in Graham Sandberg's attempt at a sympathetic description of the community in "Our Outcast Cousins in India" (B4). These efforts to describe and examine the difficulties faced by Eurasians are offset by the attitude displayed in Mrs. John Speid's *Our Last Years in India* (B3). Written by the wife of a British army officer who served in India, the narrative is typical of the prevailing stereotypes and prejudices surrounding Eurasians during the time. As the nineteenth century progressed, there were increased calls for Eurasian equality (including greater employment opportunities) within Anglo-Indian society. What was popularly termed the "Eurasian Question" or the "Eurasian Problem" also found its way into contemporary fiction. One of the earliest accounts of a biracial main character is William Browne Hockley's "The Half-Caste Daughter" (1841). This story, included in full below (B5) as a fictional counterpoint to *The Half-Caste*, describes the difficulties of Anne Berners as she tries to gain acceptance within Anglo-Indian society upon her return from England. Craik sought to raise awareness of racial issues in her novel *Olive* (1850; see B7), which provides a less sympathetic counterpoint to her discussion of a female biracial character in *The Half-Caste*. Both works consider the consequences of having mixed-race characters within England proper, and how these characters function in relation to the other British characters around them. In her portrayal of Zillah Le Poer, Craik also anticipates Philip Meadows Taylor's sympathetic rendering in *Seeta* (1872; see B6), the story of a young Indian woman who rebels against what she sees as her restrictive role as Hindu widow and mother. Choosing to live an independent life, Seeta pursues her education and her love of classical Indian literature. She eventually marries the English magistrate Cyril Brandon, and the two prove to be a good match. They live happily together until the start of the Indian

Uprising, when Seeta chooses to sacrifice herself in order to save Cyril's life.]

1. From "Half-Castes," House of Commons, Minutes of Evidence Taken before the Select Committee on the Affairs of the East India Company (16 August 1832), 300–01

Half-Castes.

The majority of half-castes reside in Calcutta. Their number has not materially increased, for the European servants of the Company[1] marry English women more generally than they did at an earlier period; and if a half-caste marry a native, the children merge in the native population; if he marry an European woman, they lose the opprobrium of being half-caste; not if a half-caste man marry an European woman, but only when a half-caste woman marries an European man. The number must have increased considerably since 1812. There are now about 20,000. The half-castes reside chiefly at the Presidencies.[2] There are very few in the interior. The disadvantages under which they labour must prevent their residence in the interior. There are but few at Bombay, from 1,000 to 2,000. In Malabar and Canara, there are about 50 or 60, the offspring of British subjects.

[...]

The half-castes partake partly of the native, and partly of the European character. They are not naturally more intelligent than the natives, but they have often a better education. They have effected greater improvements in such land as has become their property. They are in general not on a par with Europeans, either in mind or body. As a class, they are not considered to stand on a level with Europeans, but there are very many exceptions. They are treated with delicacy or vulgarity according to the character of the European with whom they have dealings. Their evidence is taken as readily as that of an European, and as much confidence is placed in it. The evidence of the half-caste is very near that of a native in point of credibility. All the feeling which the natives have against Europeans, they have also against the half-castes, whilst they probably have not the same respect for them.

---

1 The East India Company.

2 The Presidencies of colonial India were distinct areas under British administrative governance. These included the Bengal Presidency (capital at Calcutta), the Bombay Presidency (capital at Bombay), and the Madras Presidency (capital at Madras).

The half-castes are Christians, and they eat with anybody; the two great offenses in the eye of a native. So far as the Hindoos make a distinction between the half-castes and the Europeans, it is to the disadvantage of the half-castes, and they have the same feeling as between themselves and the half-castes, or even the lower order of Europeans. The prejudice the natives entertain against them arises from their being in general the offspring of low-caste women, and from their being blacker than the natives themselves, though a fair complexion is not of itself an evidence of high-caste. They are usually the children of low-caste women, or of women who have lost caste. From their want of education, and from their desertion by their fathers, with no other protection than that of their mothers, it may naturally be supposed that they must be exceedingly indolent and immoral. The females in general follow the example of their mothers. Some of the sons are employed by government, and a more meritorious or trustworthy set cannot be. Those in the public employment are respected by the natives; but it is owing to that circumstance. Some few might be admitted to situations of more trust; some are worthy of any confidence. A few have acquired landed property.

The institutions for educating them have received support from the officers and servants of the Company, but not from the Government, who have refused assistance, because, it is presumed, the objects were half-castes. At Bombay there is no public establishment for educating them; but there is a considerable school carried on by subscription, and assisted by the Government. At Calcutta there are the Military Orphan School, containing perhaps 800 boys and girls; the Parental Academic Institution, with 130 or 140 boys; the Grammar School, with 40 or 50. The children of soldiers are educated at the Lower Military Orphan School, and are sent out as drummers, &c. or apprenticed to tradesmen. There are also private schools, at which boys remain till they are 17, but they have not the means of obtaining a collegiate education. The education at Calcutta is as good as in England. The greater proportion of the half-castes must be the children of soldiers and persons in a destitute condition. There are about 1,500 educated, of whom perhaps 1,000 are employed; 500 or 600 in the public offices, and the remainder in private establishments. They are almost universally servants of the Company as clerks; and they have, with very few exceptions, confined themselves to that employment. A very superior man in the territorial department had a salary of from 50*l.* to 70*l.* a month. The half-castes have received salaries as high as 600*l.* a year, but the cases are very rare. In the police, they are employed as clerks to the magistrates, not as officers. They are eligible to all employments held by natives, but they are not much employed in them; in many of them not at all. The Government would probably be very jealous of a general employment of them, from a fear of supplanting the natives. They are allowed to enter into the service of native Princes, but not without the permission of Government. They were also employed in the irregular corps. In the Indian army, they may be employed as privates, but they are not; as drummers and musicians they are. When they are the sons of native mothers, they are excluded from the rank of officers in the Company's military, naval or civil service. The exclusion is by usage. The rule used to apply to the children of the half-castes married to Europeans; but it has been modified. Mr. Kyd, a large ship-builder at Calcutta, is a half-caste:[1] Colonel Skinner, also a half-caste, has great influence among the native population; he could raise 10,000 men at any time.[2] The natives have no objection to him on the ground of his mother having lost caste. Two or three half-castes having served their regular apprenticeship to attorneys, have been admitted as such in the Supreme Court at Calcutta. They have conducted themselves with entire propriety and integrity. Two or three are practising in the medical profession. Some have been employed as missionaries, both as teachers of schools, and as preachers of the Gospel; and have acquitted themselves well. Their influence in this respect would be increased, if they were placed in a more favourable situation. Men of education, half-castes, have gone out to India, and been compelled to return, because they could not brook the treatment they experienced. From the nature of the education the half-castes receive, and the principles in which they are brought up, they have a stronger feeling to improve their situation than Hindoos have. In the half-caste schools natives are employed to teach the native languages, but their proficiency in which the half-castes might be rendered instruments of great good to the country. The appointment of them to offices from which they are at present excluded, would raise them in the estimation of the natives, who are at all times disposed to identify them with their fathers, and it is the marked distinction which prevails that attracts their notice. Some of them are engaged in trade; some in the maritime trade of the country, to a pretty considerable extent as a beginning; no large portion of the trade between Calcutta and China

1 James Kyd (1786–1836), son of Lieutenant-General Alexander Kyd, was a master shipbuilder for the East India Company. He was educated in England and considered one of the wealthiest Eurasians of his time. A champion of Eurasian causes, Kyd (anonymously) authored *Thoughts, How to Better the Conditions of Indo-Britons* (Calcutta, 1821).

2 Lieutenant-Colonel James Skinner (1778–1841), a cavalry officer for the East India Company, was the son of a Scottish officer in the East India Company Army and an Indian noblewoman.

is conducted by them; a few are officers and captains of ships; there are some wealthy mercantile houses in Calcutta belonging to them. Many of them are qualified to hold high situations by their education. It would be extremely bad policy to admit half-castes to higher situations, for the native gentry of the country would not regard them with respect; they look down upon them very much.

2. From A.D. Rowe, *Every-day Life in India* (New York: American Tract Society, 1881), 301–02

[Adam D. Rowe, an American Lutheran minister who became known as the "Children's Missionary," arrived in India in 1874. Rowe worked as a missionary in Guntur, India, until his death from typhoid in 1882. Prior to publishing *Every-day Life in India*, Rowe authored *Talks about India for Boys and Girls* (1878) and *Talks about Mission Work in India for Boys and Girls* (1879), both of which were published in Philadelphia by the Lutheran Publication Society.]

XXXI. Eurasians.

One very important element in the conglomeration of races in India is the Eurasian or East Indian community.

The Madras Presidency alone contains about twenty thousand of these unfortunate people. We call them "unfortunate" advisedly. Sprung originally from intermarriages, and more frequently from illegal connections between the women of the lowest classes in India and their British conquerors, it is not to be wondered at that their position is a peculiarly unenviable one.

As a rule, they are thriftless in the extreme, too proud to work, but not ashamed to beg. It is a common saying in regard to them, that "they have inherited the vices of both parents and the virtues of neither."

Considering manual labor beneath them, the average Eurasian youth prefers to starve on a salary of ten rupees a month as a clerk, to learning and following a trade at which he could earn a comfortable livelihood.

In speaking of what all must admit to be the rule, we must not overlook the praiseworthy exceptions. There are also men among the Eurasians who by integrity, industry, and perseverance have risen to high and honorable places as merchants, professional men, and government officials. Those who have done so deserve the more credit for having overcome the obstacles to which most of their class succumb. It is unfortunately the case that Eurasians who have risen to places of eminence and influence too often deny the class to which they belong, and make but little effort to raise those of their brethren who are below them.

We confess that it is much easier to give advice on this subject than it would be to practise it, if placed in the position of the Eurasian who has risen above his fellows, and we incline to the doctrine that, of all men, the British themselves are the ones to take by the hand and lead upward these their unfortunate sons and daughters.

Within the last year vigorous efforts in behalf of this class have been put forth in various parts of India. "Eurasian Associations" have been formed in several centres, with the object of inducing the members of this class to turn to useful employments, as farmers, artisans, messengers, etc. The leaders, who in this case are Eurasians themselves, have great difficulties to contend with, and they ought to be heartily encouraged both by British residents and by the government.

3. From Mrs. John B. Speid, *Our Last Years in India* (London: Smith, Elder, 1862), 148

These half-caste women are the most indolent and improvident of their sex, and frequently the most flippant and conceited also. Extravagantly fond of dress, with a speciality for tawdry selection—pink crape, polka jackets, incongruously associated with red muslin bonnets, and crimson flowers, and other gorgeous apparel, that must be seen to be believed—their attractions are completed by a peculiar high-pitched voice, of unmodulated twang, and by a habit of biting out each word sharply, "topping and tailing them" (as the technical phrase is of gooseberries), with no distinction of emphasis between prepositions, conjunctions, &c. and the more dignified parts of speech. It is grievous to see how many good respectable English soldiers burden themselves with wives of this class, who usually use all their influence to prevent their ever returning to their own country. This, after a certain number of years, is an optional matter; for, on the completion of a regiment's period of Indian service, a certain number of men are permitted to volunteer for corps still in the country, a liberty of which those who have half-caste wives and families almost invariably avail themselves.

4. From Graham Sandberg, "Our Outcast Cousins in India," *The Contemporary Review* (June 1892): 880–82

[Samuel Louis Graham Sandberg (1851–1905) was a clergyman and scholar who arrived in India in 1885. He initially worked as a chaplain in Bengal, where he developed a particular interest in Tibetan geography and language. His works include *A Tibetan-English Dictionary* (1902) and the posthumous *Tibet and the Tibetans* (1906).]

Perhaps one of the more striking phenomena presented to the notice of the Englishman newly arrived in India is a certain motley section of human beings which he finds it difficult to characterise. The members of the section do not form one of the many races rightfully belonging to the land; for they hold their heads high in the presence of Hindu or Bengali, styling him "native" in tones of unusual patronage. They assuredly are not British-born; for, though some be in countenance as white as the observant newcomer himself, others of the same ilk range through every variety of shade from cream to coffee. Nevertheless, the majority of them speak the English tongue, and are known by surnames identical with those borne by scions of our loftiest houses at home—Villiers, Howard, Douglas, de Montmorency, and the rest, being each fully represented. Moreover, their religion, invariably the Christian faith, is another even stronger link. Indeed, as one looks upon this people, they seem dwelling as it were in a land of Goshen[1] which they despise, yet to which they cling; which has bred them as aliens from the womb, has enslaved them, but owns them not, affording them no sustenance. In the politest parlance, and by themselves, the strange race are denominated *Europeans*; officially they are termed *East Indians*; in general they are spoken of as *Eurasians*; while the genus Snob, unhappily now so plenteous in India, delight to apply such names as "half-caste," and even "darky," to folk at least superior to themselves. Furthermore, whereas the genuine whites resident out there belong to one of two classes, being officials in Government services or else members of the mercantile community, this nondescript section of society usually seems to resort to no settled occupation, but gives itself up to a livelihood akin to that of the birds of the air, and mainly dependent upon chance and circumstance for due supply. This, the general case, it must be allowed at the same time, is diversified by many notable and praiseworthy exceptions.

To put the matter at once upon a plain footing, the singular folk whom I wish to delineate in the present paper are the Creoles of Hindustan—the descendents, sometimes immediate, sometimes more or less remote, of conjugal unions entered into betwixt Europeans and natives of India. In such cases, here in India, as in other lands invaded

1 An area along the eastern Nile Delta in Egypt referred to in Genesis 45:9–10 as the place given to the Israelites by the Egyptian pharaoh in order to keep them separate from the native population. Because the Israelites were shepherds, they were generally disliked by the Egyptians.

by European settlers, the ratio of white to dark blood exists in a proportion variable in the individual to every possible extent. You have men and women whose faces, hardly, if at all, betray the least suspicion of Oriental taint. They are whiter to look upon than are most English persons after a single year's sojourn in the tropics. However, the black hair and dark languid eyes are rarely wanting in the fairest specimens, while experts and pseudo-experts in discrimination will always tell you that they can detect Eurasian origin without fail by means of the shape and colouring of the fingers and the finger-nails. Certain it is that fair hair, and *a fortiori* that of the red and auburn tints, may be taken as presumptive evidence that Indian blood is absent from the owner's veins. Such as are the least pronounced examples of hybridism may be possibly seven parts English and only one part native—that is, the great-grandmother may have been a pure Hindu, her husband an Englishman, and all the intervening steps in the descent to the present issue English, or at least unpronounced Eurasians. On the other hand, it has to be remembered that colour affords hardly any sure guide to the admixture of the darker race in a particular person. Eurasian parents, both of Hindu-like complexion, frequently produce offspring bearing skins irreproachable in hue. Again, the children of the same parents differ in colour to a degree hardly to be credited—the duskiest lassie may be blest with a sister endowed with the whitest of faces; and, again, a worthy couple who, proud in their fair exteriors, were congratulating themselves on having all but delivered themselves of their unpleasant ancestry, may be startled by the sudden evolution of an infant of sable visage, with the story of the past writ large upon him.

So far, however, my remarks concern what may be characterised as the *élite* of the Eurasian community. The bulk of this people are hopelessly painted with their origin in every shade belonging to the East. But it is with no intention of casting contempt upon a mere shade of colour in any human face that I refer to the fact as a melancholy circumstance. It is because the poor creatures are never allowed to forget their colour that it is to be regarded as a stigma and a stain. Not only socially, but also politically and by Government action, have they to pay the penalty of their mixed birth. As undoubted Europeans, or as undoubted Hindus, their race and complexion would prove not the slightest bar to employment and cordial recognition in the various walks of life which custom and natural adaptability have allotted to the one nation and to the other respectively. But being wholly neither of one nor of the other, they bear the disabilities of both. Their colour and antecedents disqualify them for employment as Europeans; their religion and social system debar them from participation in native industries. Despised by both races, their condition is thus often most pitiable.

5. William Browne Hockley, "The Half-Caste Daughter," from *The Widow of Calcutta; The Half-Caste Daughter; and Other Sketches* (London: D.N. Carvalho, 1841), vol. 2, 182–205

[Born and educated in England, William Browne Hockley (1792–1860) arrived in India in 1813, where he took up an appointment as a writer for the East India Company. Hockley held various administrative positions until 1824, when the British government at Bombay dismissed him under charges of bribery while he was serving as a judge. Though the charges were never officially dismissed, Hockley received a lifetime pension of £150 a year from the Company and later returned to England. His fiction, which included *Pandurang Hari* (1826), *The Zenana* (1827), *The Vizier's Son* (1831), and *The Memoirs of a Brahmin* (1843), influenced the work of many future Anglo-Indian novelists, particularly Philip Meadows Taylor.]

Forty-eight hours after the arrival of the tappal,[1] which brought him an European letter of most imposing dimensions, Lieutenant-colonel Berners, commanding a regiment of native infantry, the number of which it is not necessary to particularize, quitted the cantonment of Secunderabad,[2] and was travelling on the road to Madras with all the expedition to which money and promises could bribe a set of *dâk*[3] bearers.

The object of his journey was such as must have rendered even the velocity of a steam-carriage slow compared with his desires. He had for six weeks expected the letter on which his movements depended, and he had been in possession of leave of absence during at least half that period, for his mission brooked no delay. His daughter had arrived at the Presidency from England.

In that short sentence how much food for meditation was comprised!—How much of hope and affection was excited!—With what fondness would a father's anticipations naturally dwell on his meeting with his child! Would her beauty and graces indeed answer his proud expectations?—Did she resemble her mother? Alas! that was a question which the heart of Colonel Berners did not venture to shape to itself.

His daughter was a half-caste! However gifted by nature,—by an education which wealth had spared no cost to perfect,—by loveliness,

1 [Hockley's note:] Post.

2 [Hockley's note:] The cantonment of the Company's troops at Hyderabad. [A cantonment was the term for a military station in British India.]

3 [Hockley's note:] A relay of bearers posted at every stage, or march, as it is called in India, for those who travel by *dâk* or post.

or by intellect,—*still* a half-caste, subjected to all the stain and the stigma under which that unhappy race withers,—under which its very virtues become the instruments to render that stigma less tolerable.

Very far, therefore, were the reflections of Colonel Berners, during his long and solitary journey, from being altogether pleasurable. He knew the many mortifications which awaited the child on whom, during the last fifteen years, he had been lavishing his wealth and his affections,—mortifications from which not all his tenderness could save her. Even her letters, which had so long delighted him, had never been read without a pang far keener than that which prolonged separation would have inflicted on other fathers. How unwise, he felt, were those yearnings after the land in which her parent dwelt, which breathed in every page!—How little knew she the extent of her own misfortune!—Often had Colonel Berners meditated on the expediency of allowing her to remain longer in England, but as often the startling fact of his inability to secure for her any adequate provision in the event of his death, had compelled him to listen to the dictates of a prudence which pointed out India as the place which, with all its train of evils, at least held out the probability of her obtaining a permanent establishment. To Madras, therefore, she had been destined, and the letter which informed him of her arrival, was full of those joyous self-gratulations on being indeed in the same land with her father, which in the daughter were so natural,—to the parent so mingled with pain and bitterness.

But in the first embrace of his child, how could he remember aught but love and peace? She clung to him with all the unrestrained affection of girlhood, radiant in the beauty of seventeen,—glowing with the warm tints and flashing eyes of her oriental descent,—moving with the finished grace of her European education. In *pride* the father gazed on her, and forgot, for one brief moment, that *he* had inflicted on her the shame beneath which she was yet to bow,—that she was to shrink under the influence of *his* crime.

At present Miss Berners was a guest in the house of her father's agent, a worthy and wealthy man, but not sufficiently influential to render it advisable that his young guest should make her *dêbut* on the theatre of eastern society under his protection. Lieutenant-colonel Berners, at Madras, was only one of the fifty-two Lieutenant-colonels of Infantry who stand in the way of the promotion of their juniors. He had but one relation in the world amongst the really influential people of that worshipful community, and she was the haughty wife of a distinguished official at the head of one of the departments. He calculated, however, with great confidence, on her affording the patronage his girl would need, and trusted that, being introduced under such auspices, she would eventually form a desirable connexion. But

Colonel Berners, with his "up-country"[1] notions, had evidently reckoned without his host. He forgot that he himself was nobody amongst the elite of the Presidency,—that his country-made coatee and epaulettes were so many badges of insignificance, drawing a strong line of demarcation between himself and the high and mighty aristocracy at whose boards, by virtue of his relationship to the lady before mentioned, he was permitted to occupy occasionally a vacant seat, promoted, perhaps, to the honour, by the accident of a late refusal.

However, Colonel Berners, relying on "the force of blood," very courageously effected his entrée to the house of Mrs. Alton, on one of those days on which she had graciously condescended to withdraw the fiat of exclusion usually issued to her servants against "redcoats, and people in palanquins." This piece of good fortune was accompanied by another, highly favourable to the Colonel's designs,—the lady was alone.

After the usual greetings,—the more cordial, perhaps, for being thoroughly insincere,—Colonel Berners mentioned the arrival of his daughter, and his anxious desire to procure for her the advantage of his fair cousin's acquaintance.

"Ah! your daughter, is it?" said Mrs. Alton, with praiseworthy good humour. "I saw the name of Berners amongst the list of arrivals, but I had not the least idea that the proprietor was in any way connected with you, far less so closely. Indeed, to say the truth, Colonel,—pray forgive my *bêtise*,[2]—I am ashamed to confess, that my memory is so bad I had really forgotten you were married."

Colonel Berners looked,—what practised pen shall venture to describe *how* he looked? To Mrs. Alton, however, the expression of his face was quite intelligible, and her own gloomed instantly. "I am afraid I have trespassed on forbidden ground," she said, with a polished coldness that would have done honour to a patroness of Almack's.[3] "You will do me the justice to allow, Colonel, that after your request, it was utterly impossible I could have the remotest idea of the real state of the case."

"She is not the less my child," said the Colonel, deprecatingly, and it was all he could say at that moment.

Mrs. Alton opened her greenish eyes,—grey originally, but changed with a thick suffusion of bile, into their present verdant hue,—in an astonishment that for some seconds threatened to express itself in speechlessness.—Then was a long pause.

---

1 [Hockley's note:] A name applied to Stations remote from the Presidency.

2 A thoughtless or inappropriate remark (French).

3 Almack's Assembly Rooms, an important London social club founded in 1765 and renamed "Willis's Rooms" in 1871.

"Your child!" said the lady at length. "Very true, my dear Colonel;—there is nothing to be said against the fact, but then there *are* circumstances which, as you are well aware, it is impossible to overlook. There is really nothing in the world I would not do to oblige you, but in my position, you see, I could not effect an introduction of this kind on society without establishing a precedent. Even as it is, one is compelled to meet daily the strangest people!—And, in fact, I make it a point never to give any other person the privilege of forcing an undesirable acquaintance on me, by being exceedingly scrupulous *whom* I myself bring into notice."

Poor Colonel Berners had not, in the whole course of his previous life, felt so thoroughly humiliated! His child,—the pride of his heart,—thus contumeliously rejected by a person who owed her present position to *him*,—who had commenced her Indian career under his auspices,—and who, supposing the human heart to be not entirely *ossified*, would, it might reasonably be presumed, have rejoiced in the opportunity of repaying some part of the debt of gratitude!—There was a second pause, and during its continuance Mrs. Alton's reflections had veered in another direction, whether impelled by the expression of the Colonel's countenance or some more occult motive, it is impossible to determine.

"I am, my dear Colonel," she began, "so *very* anxious to serve you in any way I can, that waiving all my objections, I *will* call on Miss Berners, and see how we like each other. I can at least have the pleasure of receiving her at one of my small parties,"—the lady meant *second-rate parties*, and Colonel Berners was not slow in translating her less offensive expression into its very humiliating signification. However, for the sake of her on whose head his sin was now visited, he repressed his indignant feelings, and accepted the concession thus ungraciously obtained.

Mrs. Alton's promised visit was made so soon after this interview, that Colonel Berners was as near forgiving her original offence as a man could be, who felt obliged to remind himself that it was, nevertheless, unpardonable.

Very few worldly people are guilty of doing a good-natured action, at the risk of some inconvenience to themselves, without a particular motive. Mrs. Alton was actuated by *her* invisible demon in the present instance. At Madras, as elsewhere, the spirit of female rivalry runs high, in all its various shades of beauty—wit—place—and parties. Mrs. Alton's superior tact had gradually put all her antagonists *hors du combat*[1] with one exception, and that exception was made in the person of precisely the most obnoxious individual that Mrs. Alton had

1 Out of action (French).

ever inundated with her smiles and her compliments. She was one of those eternal Mrs. Brownes, who, as Mrs. Alton said, meet one at every turn of human life, in every known spot of the habitable globe. She was a *comfortable* woman,—full of mirth, and laughter, and jokes more distinguished for their humour than their brilliancy,—in short, the moral antithesis of the cold and courtly Mrs. Alton. Mrs. Browne had *just* precedence of Mrs. Alton,—the privilege of her husband's few days' seniority in the service,—and with all her good temper she had evinced a proper sense of her own position in one or two very decided instances. It followed, of course, that Mrs. Alton hated her as devoutly as ever dear friend hated dear friend. Nothing could exceed the amiable cordiality that distinguished the intercourse of the two ladies. Their greetings were of the most affectionate character,—exceeded in warmth only by the virulent abuse each lavished on the other in her own particular coterie. Mrs. Browne had just imported a daughter,—rich in all the accomplishments of the boarding-school,—a singing, dancing, laughing, romping Kitty Browne, always surrounded by a host of men, and threatening to marry most mortifyingly well. Now Mrs. Alton would have given the world to produce an eligible rival,—such a one as should throw Kitty Browne completely into shade. But her sisters were all married, and her daughters yet under the care of the Ahma,[1]—and all her aspirations after the coveted good threatened to prove ineffectual. Not that the guardianship of a young lady is generally very desirable to a woman who is herself young and well-looking enough to expect and receive a full tribute of admiration; nor could Mrs. Alton have coveted such an office, if it had not been for this odious Kitty Browne. She was so bored with the everlasting changes rung on Kitty Browne's playing,—and Kitty Browne's dancing,—and Kitty Browne's follies of all kinds,—and so distanced in the gaiety and splendour of her parties, by the superior attraction Kitty Browne bestowed on her mother's,—that she had the greatest possible desire of setting up an idol of her own. The idea of Colonel Berners's daughter was, therefore, at the first blush very agreeable, and the reaction caused by her knowledge of the irremediable stain attached to her, was proportionably violent. A few minutes, however, had sufficed to calm down her mood into that equanimity which is absolutely necessary to all those who have any object to attain. It would be as well, at all events, to see what kind of an animal the girl was,—what European education had done for her,—and whether her features and complexion were so unredeemably Asiatic, as to put the fact of her origin beyond all doubt. She did half admit the possibility of passing her on the world as a *niece* of Colonel Berners's, but this idea was checked in

1 [Hockley's note:] Nurse; the word literally signifying Mother.

its birth, by the instantaneous conviction that the Colonel himself would never sanction a deception of the kind. She had nothing left for it, therefore, but to see the girl herself, and to decide whether she could be brought forwards as a promising rival to Kitty Browne. The more she meditated on the plan, the less appalling appeared the circumstance which had at first so startled her from her propriety. Nay,—with the natural propensity of the human mind to believe that easy which it desires, and that correct which it decides on effecting,—she almost brought herself to believe, she should be able, in this particular instance, to procure the removal of the bar which excluded unmarried half-caste females from the entrée to Government House.

With such projects floating in her brain, Mrs. Alton arrived at the house where Anne Berners was staying, disposed to allow the girl credit for the full amount of any attractions she might possess,—nay, rather inclined to exaggerate them than otherwise. But even *she*,—with all this predisposition in Anne's favour,—was surprised into more real admiration than she recollected to have felt in the course of her previous life.

An eye large, brilliant, and black,—a complexion glowing with the warm tints of Italian beauties, a clear rich brunette deepening on the cheek into carnation,—a small mouth and lips of the most rosy ripeness,—scarcely closing over teeth of pearly white,—a nose partaking of the aquiline and Grecian characters, but belonging strictly to neither,—hair black, silky, and profuse,—a countenance beaming with happy youth and the hopes of a yet unclouded existence,—a form of perfect symmetry, and a stature tall enough to redeem it from that dwarfish insignificance so generally inherited by her race from their mothers, a distinctive peculiarity of their base and degraded caste;—altogether, Mrs. Alton was too much delighted with the *coup d'oeil*[1] even to venture on an expression of admiration.

Anne's manners were worthy of her beauty, which is saying much for them. Unconscious of the ordeal through which she was passing, she conversed well and easily. Mrs. Alton was enraptured, and before she shook hands with her *protegée* elect at parting, it was arranged that in two days Miss Berners should become the guest of her father's kinswoman,—an affinity now most amiably insisted on, and extended to his daughter,—for as long, Mrs. Alton said, as might suit the convenience and inclination of both parties. "In fact," she added to Colonel Berners, as he put her in her carriage, "for as long as I can keep her, which I have some suspicion will be far too short a period for my wishes."

The Colonel was delighted, and the more when he reflected how strong had been the prejudice which the charms, the graces, of his

1 A look or glance (French).

beautiful, his gifted child, had so triumphantly overcome.—Moreover, he felt relieved from much of the secret remorse with which he had been compelled to regard his own guilt as the cause of the exclusion of his daughter from the pale of her equals. He began to indulge in visions of her splendid establishment, and could not sufficiently impress on her his conviction that, in the house of his cousin, Mrs. Alton, she would find herself happily and delightfully situated beyond all she had hitherto experienced or imagined.

In that land of promise, Anne Berners soon found herself a denizen,—nay more, a star.

If admiration and flattery could confer happiness, she would have been completely blest. But what human being ever escapes the voice of the slave who warns him daily,—"*thou art mortal!*" A thousand slights,—an infinite succession of those butterfly-kicks which wear the spirit to death,—brought constantly before her the misfortune of her birth. Enchained by the strong links of prejudice, even the intelligent and the good looked down on the girl as one of a race born of shame,—whose inheritance was the vices of both parents, the virtues of neither. Willing to admit the abstract truth, that the human mind is formed by education and habit, they denied the application of it to particulars. They acted as if the accident of her birth had given a sinister bent to her heart and intellect, from which the whole subsequent circumstances of her life could not redeem her. Knowing the general inferiority of her class, they forgot that it might be traced to the successive causes of protracted companionship with the mother,—defective education,—subsequent rejection by society generally, very few Englishwomen choosing to receive a half-caste who has not covered the infamy of her descent by marriage. Was it wonderful, therefore, that marriage itself should finally be entered into chiefly as a means of escaping from this exclusion, and of acquiring in fact a social existence? —or that a connexion founded on such motives should terminate almost always in the degradation of the husband to the level of the wife, of whom he is soon ashamed, whilst, not choosing to blush openly, he affects a vulgar disregard of all opinion, which becomes at length the recklessness he had originally only simulated?—Such evils are attributed by Europeans of pure extraction to the mere fact of the mixed blood, as if its tint were the sign of the curse of Cain, entailing at once his crime and its punishment on his posterity for ever.

Mrs. Alton's triumph over Mrs. Browne and "her Kitty Browne," as she called her, was, however, quite as complete as she had calculated,—sufficiently decisive, indeed, to ensure her satisfaction with her protegée, and to render her heartily desirous of seeing Anne at the head of a comfortable establishment of her own. Mrs. Alton was too well aware of the tone of feeling pervading the whole atmosphere of

Madras society, to be annoyed at the occasional expressions of pity in behalf of Anne, to which she was obliged to listen. Having resolved that Miss Berners, as her guest, should be received every where, her exertions were incessant until her object was accomplished. Anne was not only admitted at Government House, but honoured with such particular notice as made it evident to many aspirants, that an alliance with her, so far from being an impediment in the career of their ambition, might greatly assist its success. Lovers were numerous, and proposal succeeded to proposal with such rapidity, that, as Mrs. Alton said, if her dearest Anne's head were not bewildered in deciding amidst such infinite diversity, *hers* was in conjecturing on what lucky youth that decision would ultimately rest. Colonel Berners had of necessity returned to his regiment. Previously to his departure from the Presidency, he had ventured to whisper to Mrs. Alton a regret that Anne, admired and courted as she was, had not yet effected an establishment. But Mrs. Alton reassured him, by her prognostications, that his daughter's marrying well was a certainty not one whit the less incontrovertible by being in the future tense instead of the past. Supported by such an authority, the Colonel was, as he was bound to be, content; and he awaited with cheerful patience, the letter which was to convey to him intelligence of the consummation he so devoutly wished.

With all Mrs. Alton's ambition for Anne, it had hitherto taken a general flight, nothing so uniquely desirable meeting her eye, as to distance all competitors. But at length a star appeared above the Madras horizon, to which *she* could not fail of paying her devotions, and the rather because she saw, with a watchful eye, the incense which the everlasting Mrs. Browne was offering at its shrine. A certain Sir Henry Tresham landed, adorned with all the blushing honours of the Chief Justiceship of the Presidency. He was an extremely agreeable and gentleman-like looking person *for* a Chief Justice, an advantage which might have been supposed to supersede the necessity of every other. Being a five-hundredth cousin of Mrs. Browne's, she was of course privileged to be particularly intimate with him, nor could it be deemed an unlawful spirit of monopoly in her to consider him the especial property of her Kitty. Mrs. Alton saw the game with all the superior accuracy of a looker-on, and observing the deficiency of skill in the players, boldly cut in for a hand, and very soon had the lead.

Was Anne Berners a passive instrument in the hands of her protectress—resigning heart, feelings, hopes, to her management, as if she possessed none? Anne had passed through a severe noviciate since she landed in the Indian world. She had heard the constant "Who is she?" and its terrible answer—"a half-caste!" with such intense consciousness of humiliation, as can hardly be understood by those whose happier lot has exempted them from its experience. Quite aware of the extent of her own mental and personal claims to consideration, she was doubly sensible of that pressure which continually bowed down her spirit. There was but one avenue of escape,—to become the wife of a person so influential, that the lustre of his dignity should dazzle the minds of the world—*her* world—into forgetfulness of all that his wife would wish forgotten. Having once clearly established this fact to her mind, every passion was disciplined into its proper place of subordination. Of her numerous suitors, she allowed herself to regard none with preference. If she detected her memory in dwelling on any amiable trait or attractive quality exhibited by a young man who had no other distinction, she ever afterwards treated that individual with marked coldness. She had left England artless, with all her talent,—naive, with all her polish;—six months in India, which implied six months' consciousness of the inexpiable infamy of her birth, had rendered her artificial and politic. Every day brought its lesson—an impressive one—that distinguished rank in her husband was the only shield between her and the contumely of the worthless world she despised, even whilst she could not brook its contempt. Mrs. Alton's counsels became the more oracular, in her estimation, from being identified with the results of her own experience, and she seconded her patroness's views on Sir Henry Tresham, with a skill the more effective from the display of modest indifference by which it was veiled.

"So at last the campaign is ended, my dear, and we remain in full possession of the field," said Mrs. Alton, to her protegée, the morning after Sir Henry Tresham's proposals had been formally made and accepted.

"Precisely," replied Anne, and her voice was so cold, that Mrs. Alton looked at her in amazement.

"You are practising your new character, my dear child, I perceive. But take care you 'do not o'erstep the modesty of nature.'[1] You are too grave even for the wife of a Chief Justice."

"Am I?" said Anne with a smile that had in it more of scorn than gaiety.—"I was thinking by what a direct line of causation my father's fault has led to my advancement."

"The world does not reason so deeply. They will be content to take the very evident cause of your own attractions as a most sufficient why and wherefore."

---

1 In Shakespeare's *Hamlet*, Hamlet directs the actors in his upcoming play, telling them, "Be not too tame neither, but let your own discretion be your tutor. Suit the action to the word, the word to the action, with this special observance, that you o'erstep not the modesty of nature" (3.2.19–23).

"I, at least, cannot forget. I feel that within me which, more loudly than a thousand voices, tells me I was born with feelings to participate in such household charities,—such home-attachments,—as a *purchased* wife can never share or bestow. What a destiny for a heart that has not been seared by one passion!—to which life is all untried;—*love*, yes, *love*, Mrs. Alton, but as the garden of Irêm,[1] looking at, longed for, never attained unto! Well—well—I, at least, have not wrought my own destiny, and I mean—do not look alarmed—to fill it with dignity. I might have been a happier woman, but that is a rôle quite out of the sphere of an intellectual *half-caste*;—it will be my own fault if I be not a respectable one. I am not entering into this alliance blindly;—I know what I sacrifice, and what I gain. Sir Henry is—"

"A very worthy man, child, and, which is more to the purpose, *éperdument amoureux!*"[2]

"It is my earnest hope that he will never have cause to repent his attachment. Of *my* fidelity,—nay of conduct even above suspicion,—he may be assured, for it will be the study of my existence to bequeath my children that, the want of which has been the misfortune of my life,—an honourable name.—My poor father!—What remorse he must have felt, when I landed on these shores! Knowing the habits of India so well as he did, how could he venture to bring me here, educated as I was?"

"Necessity,—necessity, *mon enfant*,[3]—which word contains the solution of half the enigmas of existence. But come,—be a little more à l'allegro. Sir Henry dines here this evening, and sadness or regret will be but a poor compliment to his disinterestedness. Do, my dear, suffer your eyes to sparkle, and your lips to smile. Only remember, how completely we have triumphed over that everlasting Kitty Browne and her horrible mother!"

Anne did remember, and she allowed her mind to dwell with complacency on an infinite succession of triumphs actual and prospective. And in that moment began the metamorphosis, which a few months perfected, of the ingenuous, vivacious, glowing Anne Berners, into the polished, correct, and heartless Lady Tresham.

6. From [Philip] Meadows Taylor, *Seeta* (1872; London: C. Kegan Paul, 1880), 48–51, 60–61, 376–78, 388–90

[Philip Meadows Taylor (1808–76) was an administrator in India and a novelist. His novels include, aside from *Seeta*, *Confessions of a*

---

1 The gardens and palace built by King Shedad in the desert of Aden.

2 Madly in love (French).

3 My child (French).

Thug (1839), *Tippoo Sultan* (1840), *Tara* (1863), and *A Noble Queen* (1878).]

From Chapter 7, "Seeta's Anklet"

Seeta was now settled at Shah Gunje.[1] She had never returned to Gokulpoor, and whatever related to her house, and to her husband's affairs, was managed by her grandfather and his agents. Narendra had the accounts of her husband's estate kept separately from his own; and it furnished a handsome income, which he held at her disposal. He had accepted the charge under trust, and associated with himself the priest Wamun Bhut, a respectable Zemindar,[2] and two bankers of the town; and thus a punchayet, or board of five persons, was formed, who audited the monthly accounts. In outward appearance Seeta was not changed; nay, she had even become more lovely. Her growing beauty, indeed, almost distressed her aunt and grandfather. Why had it been given to her? Why should such charms be vouchsafed to a widow? They watched anxiously whether, when the anniversary of her husband's death came round, she would desire to perform the duties and ceremonies of a widow in full—have her beautiful hair shorn off, and break her ornaments on the place where his body had been burned—but there was no sign of this. Once, when Aunt Ella hinted at the propriety of such a ceremony, she drew herself up, and said, proudly—

"It is not a shaven head or a coarse garment that makes a virtuous widow, Aunt Ella! What I am, I will remain. Am I to disfigure myself to shock my boy when he grows up? No! if his father's death were avenged, this might—might—be thought of; but, till then, let it not be mentioned."

So her grandfather and aunt gave the matter up, and watched her. She was not the same simple girl in character that she had been before she left them, to be moulded and influenced as they would. There was now a strange aspect of determination in her eyes which was new to them, though with it, none of her sweetness had diminished. She was quicker in decision and more fluent in speech: more keen in her discussions, especially with the priest, whose pupil she had again

1 Also given as "Shahgunje" and "Shahgunj," a town near Faizabad (Oudh), Uttar Pradesh, where a fort was located during the Indian Uprising. In his Introduction to *Seeta*, Taylor states, "My readers need not look in the map for Noorpoor and Shah Gunje, nor in the civil or military lists for my English characters, for they will not find them."

2 An official who collects land taxes in his respective district.

become—than she had used to be; and even he was often astonished and perplexed by her ability, which put his own to sharp tests.

For her child, her love amounted to a passionate devotion, which affected all who saw it very deeply. She was almost his sole attendant, anticipating every want, and never allowing him out of her sight. By this time, too, the little fellow had begun to toddle about, and even to say a word or two; and he was very handsome, for the soft, regular features and lovely eyes of his mother seemed to be blended with the more manly form of his father's countenance. Seeta was—what Indian mother is not?—fearful of the evil eye, and she had hung round her son a necklace of charms set in silver and gold, which reached to his knees. When she took him to the temple for any ceremony, the doors of her palankeen[1] were closed before she went out of her house, and never opened till she was within the sacred precincts of her teacher's temple. Between her books and the child, therefore, Seeta's time ought to have passed pleasantly; but was it so? I think not. If her grandfather had never allowed her to be educated, and if her education had not progressed to the point it had—which often caused Aunt Ella, who could not read a letter, great uneasiness—Seeta might have settled down into the dull, usual widowhood of Hindoo life; pious, absorbed in household cares, charitable, and patient, with no hope for the future, and praying that a dull mechanical life might pass away when her child grew up and entered upon his work in life.

But Seeta was not like this: the high spirit within her refused to be satisfied with what she saw in others, of whom her beloved Aunt Ella was a type. She indeed had no children; and she had no cares or aspirations. If her brother got his food regularly, if the servants were kept busy, if the poor were fed, if the household condiments, and the vermicelli in particular, were nicely prepared, if the buffaloes and cows were milked, and the butter boiled into ghee, if no ceremony, general or household, were neglected—she was satisfied; and if there were an error anywhere, she was miserable till it was corrected. Seeta could do all this as well as her aunt, and in some things she excelled her. Her grandfather would never eat vermicelli except it was prepared by her dainty fingers, and whenever he was ailing no one could please his palate but Seeta.

Not less devoted to her household duties than before she left them, Seeta was not else the same. Though she only read the sacred books and some poems and dramas, yet there were thoughts recorded in them which seemed to leap up to her own, to set her brain aching and her heart throbbing, not only at the Divine revelation, as she believed it to be, but at the language in which the strange metaphysical argu-

1 A litter that is carried on the shoulders of bearers.

ments were conveyed. Sometimes she failed to follow them; and, when she applied to her master, was often refused help! "They were mysteries which none but a Brahmin[1] should know," he would tell her; "they were not fit for the tender minds of women," and so evaded her request; but Seeta was not satisfied. There were other passages, however, in which she revelled; the descriptions of natural scenery by Kalidas and Bawa Bhut,[2] the rich episodes of the Mahabhárut and Ramayan,[3] were like new senses to her. She could hear the rushing winds and waters of the poems, watch the glowing skies, and smell the perfume of the beauteous flowers. These were realities, not inventions; and often, as she sat in her oriel window while her boy played near her, she would lay down her book, and gaze on the wooded hills, the rich cornfields, the stately groves, and the distant villages, glowing under the noontide sun, with a swelling heart and tearful eyes. And there was love too. The seers and warriors of old loved, and women loved; else who had written of love? What would it be to feel as those who so wrote and described it?—her heart gave back no echo.

Seeta had never loved. She had held her husband in respect; she was even proud of him, and he was fond of her—she was his darling! But that was not the love of the books. His life had not been her life, nor hers his. Yet such as that was not the poet's love—the pure ideal of a love which could be perfected only in Paradise! Ah! she had never known it; never would know it now; never could have known it with him! He would have gradually drawn her down to his own intellectual level, and her mind would have been stunted as it tried to grow. Now it was free! Yet who was there, among all she knew, to whom she could trace in her mind any real semblance of the divine passion? In truth, the quick, powerful intellect of her nature, so difficult to arouse, and so uncontrollable when once awakened, was leading her on by thoughts far beyond the scope of her ordinary life, and she could not stay them.

Amidst these dreams and unreal speculations, Seeta's life passed; and often as the good priest caught a glimpse of them, which he dared not follow, he would mutter to himself, "O that I had not taught her! and yet, who could restrain her ardent mind?"

---

1 In Indian society, a member of the highest caste that oversaw religious rites.

2 Kalidasa was a classical Sanskrit poet and playwright born in the fourth century CE. For "Bawa Bhut," Taylor most likely had in mind Bhavabhuti, an eighth-century Sanskrit writer of poetry and drama.

3 The *Mahabharata* and the *Ramayana* are considered two of the greatest works in ancient Indian literature. The *Ramayana* is an epic poem attributed to the Hindu Sanskrit poet Valmiki. The Sanskrit epic *Mahabharata* also includes the *Bhagavad Gita*.

From Chapter 8, "Seeta's Testimony"

At home, and since the summons, she had often felt anxious and nervous; but as her hour of trial came near, all feeling of apprehension had passed away. She might be ashamed before the magistrate; but she had a solemn duty to do, and was fearless. Then they saw the magistrate, a tall, fair young man, with a quick, strong step, pass from his private tent into the public Kucherry;[1] and after an interval of almost breathless silence among them, a messenger came forward and cried in a loud voice, "Seeta, widow of Huree Das, appear in court and give your testimony!" And the party arose and followed him.

There had been some previous depositions and other papers read, such as the verdict of the inquest, the police reports from Gokulpoor, the depositions of the goldsmiths of Noorpoor, and others; and the magistrate was examining the signature of Seeta's summons with a curious interest. The characters, "Seeta, widow of Huree Das," were very delicate and beautiful; he had never seen such before, and he marvelled that a woman could have written them. "Surely they are not her own," he said to his Serishtadar, or head officer. "No woman could write like this."

"She is a strange girl," he replied, "and people say she is very learned. Yes, the signature is her own doubtless; no man could write like that." And hearing this, Cyril Brandon only wondered the more. "What would she be like?" In his own mind he had concluded that Seeta would be in no wise different from other women of her class; quiet, modest, and timid, yet in no degree interesting; and having directed her to be called in, he looked round.

[...]

As Seeta and her aunt entered with the priest and her grandfather, the tent door was somewhat darkened; but as she took the place assigned to her, the light from without fell full upon her, and the young magistrate thought he had never seen any woman more lovely. He could, indeed, scarcely suppress an exclamation of surprise; but he checked himself, and holding up the summons, said gently, "Seeta, the widow of Huree Das, is this your signature?"

"It is mine," she said modestly, raising her eyes to his. "With my own hand I wrote it, and I come of my own free will."

The large dewy eyes were soft and pleading, but not irresolute, and the girl was quite calm. Seeta had dressed herself in a rich silk saree[2]

1 Court. Also given as "kutchery."

2 A sari is a traditional Indian garment made of lightweight cloth that is folded around the body, forming a skirt and draping over the shoulder or head.

of a green colour, shot with crimson, which had heavy borders and ends of gold thread, and the end, which she had passed over her head, fell on her right arm and contrasted vividly with its fair colour and rounded outline. If her features were not exactly regular, they were very sweet and full of expression; her eyes were large and soft, of that clear dark brown which, like a dog's, is always so loving and true. If the mouth were a shade too full for exact symmetry, it was mobile and expressive, and the curves of the upper lip constantly varied. For a native woman, Cyril Brandon had never seen any one so fair or of so tender a tone of colour. Such, he remembered, were many of the lovely women of Titian's pictures[1]—a rich golden olive, with a bright carnation tint rising under the skin—and Seeta's was like them. One in particular came to his memory like a flash—the wife of the Duc d'Avalos, in the Louvre picture; or Titian's Daughter, carrying fruits and flowers, at Berlin. He could not see much of Seeta's figure; but the small, graceful head, the rounded arm, the tiny foot, the graceful movement of the neck, and her springy lithe step as she had entered the tent, assured him that it could not be less beautiful than the face. It was curious, too, that all present in the court had been excited, and a sound as if of a long-drawn breath had gone out even from some of the prisoners, who still sat on the floor.

From Chapter 45, "Faithful unto Death"

So there was a pleasant party at the Judge's; and much talk and speculation ensued at dinner upon what might be going on elsewhere. After the ladies had retired for a short time, the gentlemen joined them in the drawing-room, and the piano was opened and the music began as usual. Never were the parties in better voice, for their good spirits gave them unusual energy; and it was a treat to sing there after so long. Seeta had listened for some time, sitting in Grace's boudoir which adjoined the drawing-room; and she had gone home to dress for the night ride with Cyril, for the patrols were still continued. She changed her clothes and went up on the terrace of part of her cottage, and was sitting by herself thinking much, when Buldeo suddenly called to her from below, "Come down! come down! I have seen them! Quick, lady!" And almost as he spoke, looking towards the shrubbery near the road, she saw distinctly a body of men moving silently and rapidly. In an instant she was flying down the steps with her utmost speed and up the gravel walk to the Judge's house. Entering by the

1 Tiziano Vecellio (c. 1488–1576), known as Titian in English, was a famed member of the Venetian School of painters. He is now considered to be the greatest Venetian artist of the sixteenth century.

back, she ran on through the house, and burst into the drawing-room, where Grace and Cyril were singing the old "Dimmi che m' ami, ancor."[1] All looked strangely at her for a moment; but terror was in her face, she was out of breath and could only cry out, "Fly! get to the fort, the rebels are on us," when shouts arose outside, and a volley was fired through the windows, shattering the glass and frames, and knocking plaster from the walls.

No one, then, went about without arms; and there were loaded guns, revolvers, and swords in the corners of the room; each snatched his own weapons, and as yet no one was harmed. If it had been possible, the officers would have held the drawing-room till succour should reach them from the water-gate; but it was not to be done, the attacking party had at once fired the thatch in several places, and the blaze spread over the garden, increasing every instant. "Look to the ladies, gentlemen," cried the Brigadier sharply; "we must cover them." There was now a great clamour without, for the Judge's police guard and Cyril's, with the Rahtores,[2] had struck in manfully; but they were too few to stop the attack at once.

Cyril was supporting Grace, who had clung to him; and Seeta, whose presence of mind seemed to be rising, also put her arm round her, and led her on. Mr. Mostyn and one of the other officers hurried on Mrs. Mostyn. They had already got down the steps, and Cyril was following, when Azráel Pandé,[3] more terrible to look on than ever, his eyes staring, and his livid shattered face convulsed with passion, sprang suddenly on him from a corner of the verandah, with his spear. Cyril parried the thrust, and made a cut with his sword in return, which was caught on his spear by the Dacoit,[4] when at that instant a chance shot struck Cyril in the right arm, and his sword dropped. He

1 "Tell me again that you love me," spoken by Faust to Marguerite in Act III of Charles Gounod's (1818–93) opera *Faust*, which premiered in Paris in 1859.

2 The Rathores make up one of the Rajput ("son of a king") clans. They trace their lineage from the Suryavansha (Solar) Dynasty of ancient India, also known as the Solar Race of Rajputs. The Rathores were known for their loyalty to the British during the Indian Uprising.

3 Taylor notes in his Introduction that "Pandé is not, as might be imagined, a surname. It is one of the divisions of Brahmins of Oudh and Bahar, as Doobé, Chowbé, Tewarree, Missr, etc., etc., which are very numerous." He continues: "In Azráel Pandé I have endeavoured to depict the character of the rebel and treasonable emissaries of the time. Malignant and persistent, they were led on by blind hatred and religious fanaticism, to the instigation and commission of crimes at which humanity shudders; and in Azráel's address to the Sepoy delegates at Barrackpoor I think I have included all the 'wrongs' under which the Bengal Sepoys professed to suffer."

4 Bandit.

was entirely at his enemy's mercy. "Jey Kalee Mata!" shouted Azráel. "Dog of a Feringee![1] No escape now for thee," and as he drew back his deadly weapon to strike, Cyril heard a cry—it was not a scream—and Seeta had rushed before him, receiving the blow in her breast. Then Captain Hobson, who had tried to save Seeta, or, as he first thought, Cyril, plunged his sword into the ruffian's heart, who, writhing impaled upon the weapon for an instant, fell to the ground and was despatched, if indeed he lived, by Buldeo, with repeated thrusts of his own spear.

It was all the work of a moment, and while other combats were going on in the verandah and in the garden, and Luchmun Singh and the Rahtores, with the police, were striking in with their war cries, Cyril stood for a moment stunned and bewildered. His right arm was pierced and nearly useless: but he tried to raise up Seeta, while Grace Mostyn, who had not lost her presence of mind, was endeavouring to staunch the blood with her dress and her handkerchief. Then Hobson and Buldeo gently took up the wounded girl between them, and carried her down the steps, Cyril following, and Grace holding her hand. For a moment Seeta's eyes opened, and she said to Grace, faintly, "Run, save yourself—let me die here," and again relapsed into insensibility. So they carried her down the garden, till they were in some degree safe; then Buldeo undid his waistcloth, and they put Seeta into it, and with some others carried her on gently to the water-gate, where Mr. Mostyn, his wife, and others were preceding them.

As the officer at the gate saw the outbreak of the disturbance at Mr. Mostyn's, he had dashed down with half his men to the rescue; but he was too late. Dismayed by the death of their leader, and by the loss they had already sustained from the spirited defence of the officers and the guards, as well as from several discharges of grape[2] which the watchful sergeant had fired at the crowd on Mr. Brandon's lawn, now perfectly distinct under the glare from his burning house, and Seeta's cottage, the rebel Sepoys[3] and their companions fled in confusion; and with the English guard covering the retreat of the party, in a few minutes the gate was entered and closed. Except a few hurried mournful words, no one spoke, as the sad procession wound up the path to the tower, lighted by the blazing houses, little heeding the rattle of

1 Firangi is a Hindu term for a European or other foreigner.

2 Grapeshot is a grouping of small metal balls clustered together, resembling a cluster of grapes.

3 Indian soldiers serving in the British Army. Because many Sepoys in the East India Company's army rebelled against the British during the Indian Uprising of 1857–58, the revolt came to be known as the Sepoy Rebellion or the Sepoy Mutiny.

musketry, and the guns from the cavalier, which showed that the attack on the Judge's house had been a feint for a more serious and obstinate one in front, than had ever occurred before.

From Chapter 47, "Shah Gunje"

Some weeks had passed, wearily and sadly. At the moment, and, indeed, for many days after Seeta's death, Cyril Brandon had been stunned by the loss of one who had grown to be more his companion and friend than he had ever believed possible; and now, ensued the aching void, which there was nothing to fill up. He missed Seeta at every turn, and in every occupation she had shared with him. At first, their lives had not had much in common, perhaps; but the ardent nature of Seeta's mind had already overcome many hindrances to more perfect communion. In her indefatigable studies she had been chiefly guided by Grace Mostyn, whose serene and delicate feeling had been reflected in her pupil. It was almost unaccountable to Cyril and her friends, how much, and how rapidly, Seeta had learned during the last four months; how much her capacity had been enlarged, and her sense of comprehension vivified by her enthusiasm in her new pursuits. She had, indeed, but one incentive to exertion: the desire to be, what she felt she ought to be, as Cyril's wife. Not the mere Hindoo girl, whom no one could know but her husband; but one who, in time, might take her place openly in the world, and of whom he should never be ashamed. And it had seemed to Grace and her sister that this might come to be; but that it would necessarily be impossible so long as Seeta retained her Hindoo faith and her customs.

Would she ever relinquish them? That, indeed, had been a subject of anxious discussion between all who loved Seeta; but even Mrs. Pratt, whose education and experience as a missionary gave her more weight and perception than Mrs. Mostyn or Grace, had hesitated to make any decided attempt at conversion. Seeta's mind was not yet prepared for the change. She could not throw off caste. She could not dissever herself from her old associations and her deep love for those who remained at Shah Gunje. She could not at once abandon the old belief in which she had been reared, and the deep and often grand metaphysical arguments by which it was supported. Before these, the simplicity of Christian truth had, at first, indeed, appeared childish, if not contemptible; and yet how they had perceptibly grown upon her! How they were urging her on to take one final, irrevocable step, we already know in part, but not entirely. Nor is it needful for me to lay bare the struggles of that loving, pious heart more than I have already done in these imperfect pages. Such struggles, even in Christian hearts yearning to feel the truth, are often long and terrible; how much more, then, those of a heathen, with intellect and education powerful enough to understand it, and yet with every consideration, before held most sacred and precious, not only to be risked, but abandoned entirely for a new faith, and altogether new affections and associations. If she renounced Hindooism, she should be a stranger in her grandfather's home. She could not eat with them, or live with them, at all, as she had used to do. They might reproach her, and refuse to see her; and Wamun Bhut, her revered preceptor, would be grieved to the heart. Her old associates would despise her, for she knew how Christianity was esteemed among them—nay, how she had esteemed it herself, hardly a year ago. If Cyril died—and he might die before her—and she were a Christian, who could receive her, when her caste was gone? No penance, no fine, no entreating of the guild, or the Brahmins at Benares, could restore what she had designedly given up. She must live alone, as an outcast: and if she died, who would even bury her?

I say these and a thousand other thoughts were daily passing through Seeta's mind, as the time went on, and the weakening of the old bulwarks of her faith was progressing; and, perhaps, in this respect, Seeta is only a type of thousands and thousands of her own countrymen and women, who feel the truth, and who, until some unforeseen crisis in their lives arises, dare not make the final plunge which not only severs them from all they love, honour, and respect in life, but makes them social outcasts—utterly despised and rejected by their people, even to the refusal of a cup of cold water. Too many among us blame the hardness of the heathen, and call their belief in their own faith by very ugly names; but I think the utmost bound of charity needs to be extended to them when we think on—if we can at all estimate—the force of the reality of struggles like Seeta's. And yet they who watched by the dying girl in that memorable night, knew how near she was in faith to God, in whom she trusted as a child. Would she ever have accepted baptism? They could not tell, for none had dared to ask. They had been content to watch the mental struggle, and to comfort and encourage Seeta as well as they could.

Yet towards becoming a Christian, the advantages, in a worldly point of view, appeared by far more decided than in continuing as she was. Mrs. Pratt had put Seeta's position before her more plainly than any one, except Cyril himself, who had never concealed it. As a Christian, he would marry her by Christian rites. No one could then deny her right to social rank and position. She might go to England, and visit Lady Hylton. She might even, if Cyril's brother died, be a Lady Hylton too, honoured and respected. If she bore children to her husband, they would no longer have a stigma of illegitimacy according to English law; and had she not of her love, of her faith and constancy, cast her lot with a Christian? So it would seem to be her duty to belong to her husband's faith: to abandon all else, loving and venerating it, never so much. Had she any right to refuse what she knew her husband would hail with delight? Then she and Grace would be indeed sisters, for Mrs. Mostyn had said playfully one day, that she and Mrs. Pratt must be her godmothers. All this Seeta knew, yet it had not dazzled her, not helped to still the tempest in her heart, in which no worldly motives were engaged. Yet the crisis was nigh, and a few, a very few days perhaps, would most probably have decided the question, which was solved otherwise, now, and for ever.

7. From Dinah Mulock Craik, *Olive* (London: Chapman and Hall, 1850), 61–72, 183–93, 194–96

From Volume 2, Chapter 3

Day by day, as her spirit strengthened and her genius developed, Olive's existence seemed to brighten. Her domestic life was full of many dear ties, the chief of which was that wild devotion, less a sentiment than a passion, which she felt for her mother. Her intellectual life grew more intense and all-vivifying; while she felt the stay and solace of having one pursuit to occupy the whole aims and desires of her future. Also, it was good for her to dwell with the enthusiastic painter and his meek contented little sister; for she learnt thereby that life might pass not merely in endurance, but in peace, without either of those blessings which in her early romance she deemed the chief of all—beauty and love. She felt that worth and genius were above them both.

The lesson was impressed more deeply by a little incident that chanced about this time.

Miss Vanbrugh sometimes took Olive with her on those little errands of charity which were not unfrequent with the gentle Meliora.

"I wish you would come with me to-day," she said once, "because, to tell the truth, I hardly like to go alone."

"Indeed!" said Olive, smiling, for the little old maid was as brave as a lion among those gloomiest of all gloomy lanes. She would traverse them even in dark nights, and this was a sunny spring morning.

"I am not going to see an ordinary poor person, but that strange foreign-looking woman—Mrs. Manners, who is one of my brother's models sometimes—you know her?"

"Scarcely; but I have seen her pass through the hall. Oh, she was a grand, beautiful woman, like an Eastern queen. You remember it was she from whom Mr. Vanbrugh painted the 'Cleopatra.' What an eye she had, and what a glorious mouth!" cried Olive, waxing enthusiastic.

"Poor thing! Her beauty is sadly wasting now," said Meliora. "She seems to be slowly dying, and I shouldn't wonder if it were of sheer starvation; those models earn so little. Yesterday she fainted as she stood—Michael is so thoughtless. He had to call me to give her some wine, and then we sent the maid home with her. She lives in a poor place, Jane says, but quite decent and respectable. I shall surely go and see the poor creature; but she looks such a desperate sort of woman, her eyes glare quite ferociously sometimes. She might be angry—so I had rather not be alone, if you will come, Miss Rothesay?"

Olive consented at once; there was in her a daring romance which, putting all sympathy aside, would have quite gloried in such an adventure.

They walked for a mile or two until they reached a miserable street by the river-side; but Miss Meliora had forgotten the number. They must have returned, their quest unsatisfied, had not Olive seen a little girl leaning out of an upper window,—her ragged elbows on the sill, her wild elf-like black eyes watching the boats up and down the Thames.

"I know that child," Olive said; "it is the poor woman's. She left it in the hall one day at Woodford-cottage, and I noticed it from its black eyes and fair hair. I remember, too—for I asked—its singular and very pretty name, *Christal*."

Talking thus, they mounted the rickety staircase, and inquired for Mrs. Manners. The door of the room was flung open from without, with a noise that would have broken any torpor less deep than that into which its wretched occupant had fallen.

"*Ma mie*[1] is asleep; don't wake her or she'll scold," said Christal, jumping down from the window, and interposing between Miss Vanbrugh and the woman who was called Mrs. Manners.

She was indeed a very beautiful woman, though her beauty was on a grand scale. She had flung herself, half-dressed, upon what seemed a heap of straw with a blanket thrown over. As she lay there, sleeping heavily, her arm tossed above her head, the large but perfect proportions of her form reminded Olive of the reclining figure in the group of the "Three Fates."

But there was in the prematurely old and wasted face something that told of a wrecked life. Olive, prone to romance-weaving, wondered whether nature had in a mere freak invested an ordinary low-born woman with the form of the ancient queens of the world, or whether within that grand body lay ruined an equally grand soul.

---

1 "My dear" or "my love" (French).

Miss Meliora did not think about anything of the sort; but merely that her brother's dinner-hour was drawing near, and that if poor Mrs. Manners did not wake, they must go back without speaking to her.

But she did wake soon—and the paroxysm of anger which seized her on discovering that she had intruding guests, caused Olive to shrink back almost to the staircase. But brave little Miss Vanbrugh did not so easily give up her charitable purpose.

"Indeed, my good woman, I only meant to offer you sympathy, or any help you might need in your illness."

The woman refused both, in an accent that to Olive seemed rather Spanish—or perhaps she fancied so, because the dark face had a Spanish, or Creole cast. "I tell you, we want for nothing."

"*Ma mie!* I am so hungry!" said little Christal, in a tone between complaint and effrontery. "I will have something to eat."

"You should not speak so rudely to your mother, little girl," interposed Miss Meliora.

"My mother! No, indeed; she is only *ma mie*. My mother was a rich lady, and my father a noble gentleman."

"Hear her, Heaven! oh, hear her!" groaned the woman on the floor.

"But I love *ma mie* very much—that's when she's kind to me," said Christal; "and as for my own father and mother, I don't remember them at all, for, as *ma mie* says, they were drowned together in the deep sea, years ago."

"I would they had been—I would they had been," was the muttered answer, as Mrs. Manners clutched the child—a little, thin-limbed, cunning-eyed girl, of eight or ten years old—and pressed her to her breast, with a strain more like the gripe of a lioness than a tender woman's clasp.

Then she fell back quite exhausted, and took no more notice of anybody. Meliora's easily-roused compassion forgot Mr. Vanbrugh's dinner, and all things else, in making a few charitable arrangements, that resulted in a comfortable tea for little Christal and "*ma mie.*"

Sleep had again overpowered the sick woman, who appeared to be slowly dying of that anomalous disease called decline, in which the mind is the chief agent of the body's decay. Meanwhile, Miss Vanbrugh talked in an undertone to little Christal, who, her hunger satisfied, stood, her finger in her mouth, watching the two ladies with her fierce black eyes—the very image of a half-tamed gipsy. Indeed, Miss Meliora seemed rather uneasy, and desirous to learn more of her companions, for she questioned the child closely.

"And is the person you call *ma mie* any relation to you?"

"The neighbours say she must be my aunt, from the likeness. I don't know."

"And her name is Mrs. Manners—a widow, no doubt; for I remember she was in very respectable mourning when she first came to Woodford Cottage," said Meliora, who, having thus far drawn on her lively imagination, deeply sympathized with the supposed heroine of her fanciful tale.

"Poor young creature!" she continued, sitting down beside the object of her compassion, who was, or seemed, asleep. "How hard to lose her husband so soon! and I dare say she has gone through great poverty—sold one thing after another to keep her alive. Why, I declare," added the simple and unworldly Meliora, who could make a story to fit anything, "poor soul! she has even been forced to part with her wedding-ring."

"I never had one—I scorned it!" cried the woman, leaping up with a violence that quite confounded the painter's sister. "Do you come to insult me, you smooth-tongued English lady? Ah, you shrink away—I am too vile for your presence, am I?"

"I don't know anything about you, indeed," said Meliora, creeping to the door; while Olive, who, as yet untouched by human passion, could not understand the mystery of half she witnessed, stood simply looking on in wonder—almost in admiration. To her there seemed a strange beauty, like that of a Pythoness,[1] in the woman's attitude and mien.

"You know nothing of me? Then you shall know. I come from a country where are thousands of young maidens, whose blood, half-Southern, half-European, is too pure for slavery, too tainted for freedom. Lovely, and taught all accomplishments that can ennoble beauty, brought up delicately, in wealth and luxury, they yet have no higher future than to be the white man's passing toy—cherished, mocked, and spurned."

She paused; and Miss Vanbrugh, astonished at this sudden outburst, in language so vehement, and above her apparent sphere, had not a word to say. The woman continued:

"I but fulfilled my destiny. How could such as I hope to bear an honest man's honest name? So, when my fate came upon me, I cast all shame to the winds, and lived out my life. I followed my lover across the seas; I clung to him, faithful in my degradation; and when his child slept on my bosom, I looked at it, and was almost happy. Now, what think you of me, virtuous English lady?" cried the outcast, as she tossed back her cloud of dark crisped hair, chief token of her

---

1 A prophetess or soothsayer in the tradition of the Pythia, the female oracles in the Temple of Apollo at Delphi.

Quadroon blood,[1] and fixed her eyes sternly, yet mockingly, upon her visitors.

Poor Miss Vanbrugh was conscious of but one thing, that this scene was most unmeet for a young girl; and that if once she could get Olive away, all future visits to the miserable woman should be paid by herself alone. Yet still she had the charity to say, in forbearing and half-disguised words,

"I will see you another day, Mrs. Manners, but we cannot really stay now. Come away, my dear Miss Rothesay."

And she and her charge quitted the room. Apparently, their precipitate departure still further irritated the poor creature they had come to succour; for as they descended the stairs, they heard her repeatedly shriek out Olive's surname, in tones so wild, that whether it was meant for rage or entreaty they could not tell.

From Volume 3, Chapter 9

A solemn, anxious feeling stole over her. Ere breaking the seal, she lingered long; she tried to call up all she remembered of her father—his face—his voice—his manners. Very dim everything was! She had been such a mere child until he died, and the ten following years were so full of action, passion, and endurance of much-tried womanhood, that they made the old time look pale and distant. She could hardly remember how she used to feel then, least of all how she used to feel towards her father. She had loved him, she knew, and her mother had loved him, ay, long after love became only memory. He had loved them, too, in his quiet way. Olive thought, with tender remembrance, of his kiss on that early morning when, for the last time, he had left his home. And for her mother! Often, during Mrs. Rothesay's declining days, had she delighted to talk of the time when she was a young happy wife, and of the dear love that Angus bore her. Something, too, she hinted of her own faults, which had once shadowed that love, and something Olive's own childish memory told her that this was true. But she repelled the thought, remembering that her father and mother were now together before God.

At length, with an effort, she opened the letter. She started to see its date—the last night Captain Rothesay ever spent at home—the night, which of all others, she had striven to remember clearly, because they were all three so happy together, and he had been so kind, so

1 A term used to describe people with mixed African and European ancestry. Someone described as a "Quadroon" (derived from the French "quarteron") implied that the person had a quarter of African ancestry, meaning one biracial (African/Caucasian) parent and one white/European parent.

loving, to her mother and to her. Thinking of him on this wise, with a most tender sadness, she began to read:

"OLIVE ROTHESAY—MY DEAR CHILD!

"It may be many—many years—(I pray so, God knows!) before you open this letter. If so, think of me as I sit writing it—or rather as I sat an hour ago—by your mother's side, with your arms round my neck. And, so thinking of me, consider what a fierce struggle I must have had to write as I am going to do—to confess what I never would have confessed while I lived, or while your mother lived. I do it, because remorse is strong upon me; because I would fain that my Olive—the daughter who may comfort me, if I live—should, if I die, make atonement for her father's sins. Ay, sins. Think how I must be driven, thus to humble myself before my own child—to unfold to my pure daughter that—But I will tell the tale plainly, without any exculpation or reserve.

"I was very young when I married Sybilla Hyde. God be my witness! I loved her then, and in my inmost heart I have loved her evermore. Remember, I say this—hear it, as if I were speaking from my grave—Olive, *I did love your mother*. Would to Heaven she had loved me, or shown her love, only a little more!

"Soon after our marriage I was parted from my wife for some years. You, a girl, ought not to know—and I pray may never know—the temptations of the world and of man's own nature. I knew both, and I withstood both. I came back, and clasped my wife to the most loving and faithful heart that ever beat in a husband's breast. I write this even with tears—I, who have been so cold. But in this letter—which no eye will ever see until I and your mother have lain together long years in our grave—I write as if I were speaking, not in my own worldly self, but as I should speak then.

"Well, between my wife and me there came a cloud. I know not whose was the fault—perhaps mine, perhaps hers; or, it might be, both. But there the cloud was—it hung over my home, so that I could find therein no peace, no refuge. It drove me to money-getting excitement, to amusement—at last to crime!

"In the West Indies there was one who had loved me, in vain,—mark you, I said *in vain*,—but with the vehemence of her southern blood. She was a Quadroon lady—one of that miserable race, the children of planters and slaves, whose beauty is their curse, whose passion knows no law except a blind fidelity. And, God forgive me! that poor wretch was faithful unto me.

"She followed me to England without my knowledge. Little she had ever heard of marriage; she cared nothing for mine. I did not love her—not with a pure heart as I loved Sybilla. But I pitied her. Sometimes I turned from my dreary home—where no eye brightened at mine, where myself and my interests were nothing—and I thought of this woman, to whom I was all the world. My daughter Olive, if ever you be a wife, and would keep your husband's love, never let these thoughts darken his spirit! Give him your whole heart, and he will ask no other. Make his home sweet and pleasant to him, and he will not stray from it. Bind him round with cords of love—fast—fast. Oh, that my wife had had strength so to encircle me!

"But she had not; and so the end came! Olive, you are not my *only* child.

"I have no desire to palliate my sin. Sin, I know it was, heavy and deadly; against God's law, against my trusting wife, and against that hapless creature on whom I brought a whole life-time of misery. Ay, not on her alone, but on that innocent being who has received from me nothing but the heritage of shame, and to whom in this world I can never make atonement. No man can! I felt this when she was born. It was a girl, too—a helpless girl. I looked on the little face, sleeping so purely, and remembered that on her brow would rest through life a perpetual stain; and that I, her father, had fixed it there! Then there awoke in me a remorse which can never die. For, alas, Olive, I have more to unfold! My remorse, like my crimes, was selfish at the root, and I wreaked it on her, who, if guilty, was less guilty than I.

"One day I came to her, restless, bitter in spirit, unable to hide the worm that was continually gnawing at my heart. She saw it there, and her proud spirit rose up in anger; she poured on me a torrent of reproachful words. I answered them as one who had erred like me was sure to answer. Poor wretch! I reviled her as having been the cause of my misery. When I saw her in her fury, I contrasted her image with that of the pale, patient, trusting creature I had left that morning—my wife, my poor Sybilla—until, hating myself, I absolutely loathed *her*—the enchantress who had been my undoing. With her shrill voice yet pursuing me, I precipitately left the house. Next day mother and child had disappeared! Whither, I knew not; and I never have known, though I left no effort untried to solve a mystery which made me feel like a *murderer*.

"Nevertheless, a feeling rests with me that they are still alive—these wretched two. If I thought not so, I should almost go mad at times.

"Olive, have pity on your father, and hearken to what I implore. Whilst I live, I shall continue this search—but I may die without having had the chance of making atonement. In that case I entreat of my daughter Olive, who will, I foresee, grow up noble and virtuous among women, to stand between her father and his sin. If you have no other ties—if you never marry, but live alone in the world—seek out and protect that child! Remember, she is of your own blood—*she*, at least, never wronged you. In showing mercy to her, you do so to me, your father; who, when you read this, will have been for years among the dead, though the evil that he caused may still remain unexpiated. Oh! think that this is his voice crying out from the dust, beseeching you to absolve his memory from guilt. Save me from the horrible thought, now haunting me evermore, that the being who owes me life may one day heap curses on her father's name!

"Herewith enclosed you will find instructions respecting an annuity I wish paid to—to the woman. It was placed in ——'s bank by Mr. Wyld, whom, however, I deceived concerning it—I am now old enough in the school of hypocrisy. Hitherto the amount has never been claimed.

"Olive, my daughter, forgive me! Judge me not harshly. I never would have asked this of you while your mother lived—your mother, whom *I loved*, though I wronged her so grievously. In some things, perhaps, she erred towards me; but I ought to have shown her more sympathy, and have dealt gently with her tender nature, so unlike my own. May God forgive us both!—God, in whose presence we shall both be, when you, our daughter, read this record. And may He bless you evermore, prays your loving father,

ANGUS ROTHESAY.

"In my shame, I have not yet written the name of that hapless woman. It was Celia Manners. To the child, I remember, she gave a remarkable name—I think, that of *Christal*."

It ceased—this voice from the ten years' silent grave of Angus Rothesay. His daughter sat motionless, her fixed eyes blindly outgazing, her whole frame cold and rigid, frozen into the likeness of a statue of stone.

From Volume 3, Chapter 10

Rivetted by an inexplicable influence, Olive had read the letter through, without once pausing or blenching;—read it as though it had been some strange romance of misery, not relating to herself at all. She felt unable to comprehend or realise it, until she came to the name—"Christal." Then the whole truth burst upon her, wrapping her round with a cold horror, and, for the time, paralysing all her faculties. When she awoke, the letter was still in her hand, and from it still there stood out clear the name, which had long been a familiar word. Therefore, all this while, destiny had been leading her to work out her father's desire. The girl who had dwelt in her household for months, whom she had tried to love, and generously sought to guide, was—*her sister.*

But what a chaos of horror was revealed by this discovery! Olive's first thought was of her mother, who had showered kindness on this child of shame; who, dying, had unconsciously charged her to "take care of Christal."

With a natural revulsion of feeling, Olive thrust the letter from her. Its touch seemed to pollute her fingers.

"Oh, my mother—my poor, wronged mother!—well for you that you never lived to see this day. You—so good, so loving, so faithfully remembering him even to the last. But I—I have lived to shrink with abhorrence from the memory of my own father."

Suddenly she stopped, aghast at thinking that she was thus speaking of the dead—the dead from whom her own life had sprung.

Appendix C: The Victorian Governess

[The social and financial status of the Victorian governess was a topic of debate throughout the nineteenth century. "Hints on the Modern Governess System" (Appendix C1) and Sarah Lewis's "On the Social Position of Governesses" (C2), both of which appeared in *Fraser's Magazine*, discuss the role of education, fair pay, and standardization in improving the profession as a whole, thereby improving the conditions of women who worked as governesses. Emily Peart's *A Book for Governesses* (C3) provides an example of the many instructional treatises designed to prepare young women for life as governesses, especially women who unexpectedly found themselves seeking employment due to financial obligations or other family misfortune. The authenticity of both Lewis's and Peart's work is supported by the fact that both women previously worked as governesses. Two of Charlotte Brontë's letters, from 1839 and 1841 (C4), also provide a personal perspective on the difficulties experienced by governesses. In her correspondence, Brontë privately admitted that she was not suited to such employment, and she frequently expresses her unhappiness and loneliness while serving as a private governess. Craik examined the life of a governess in her tale *Bread upon the Waters* (C5), which she published to benefit the Governesses' Benevolent Institution (see Introduction, p. 27, note 1). After being forced to leave her father's home after the arrival of a manipulative stepmother, the main character, Felicia Lyne, accepts work as a governess in order to support herself and her two brothers. Felicia perseveres through financial hardship and loneliness until she finds security working as a private governess for the aristocratic Airlie family.]

1. From "Hints on the Modern Governess System," *Fraser's Magazine* (November 1844): 572–83

Now, when that cry of women after knowledge pierced the air, a thousand sprang up, mushroomwise, in a night, to answer it. Mothers who had only read their bibles and receipt-books found themselves unprepared for the emergency—we have so little patience, so little foresight. Then, teaching, that holy vocation of a woman, became a trade. An universal demand creates its own supply. Here was a tempting opening to all aspiring women, who were free to try a new field; the unmarried daughters of the gentry left with scanty portions, had, till now, been content to eke out their small incomes in trade; many were the gentlewomen, in our great-grandmothers' days, who lived in honoured independence, though they kept small shops, to which their old friends resorted. They did not lose caste because they sat for part of the day behind the counter. However, this refuge grew insecure from the outward pressure of public opinion in favour of refinement. The vast spread of colonisation at this juncture drew many bold spirits among the men from the warehouse. Women shared in the growing distaste for the ell-wand and the steel-yard.[1] Many left their quiet homes for the school-rooms of halls and castles. As they mounted the stair, others came from a lower rank, and filled the vacant steps. The restless rage to push on had stirred all classes. Those who, disappointed in their new stand, looked wistfully back to the old, found that when they would return they could not. There was no place left for them but that which they had chosen. Like much else, it looked best from a distance. Here, then, was a whole class of women driven into a new line, for which they had received no fitting preparation. As America and the Indies were filled by swarms of adventurers, marriage necessarily decreased. There was such an over-plus of single women that the old order of things was subverted. Women must have bread to eat as well as men. If they have no husbands to toil for them, they must win food for themselves. They found, if they would not sink in the scale, they must work with their heads, and not with their hands. Must! oh, the ruthlessness of necessity! We know the fate of the weed when mighty waters rush together. The new generation, thirsting to be taught, found teachers at their mercy, hanging between two ranks. Do the weak desire to learn what they may expect from the strong? Let them ponder deeply the governess system of the present day. This was the watch-word, "Teach us on our own terms, or work, and cease to be gentlewomen." To the newly risen race of governesses, even such equivocal gentility was preferable to a second change, though it was to be gained at the price of isolation. Time was when the daughters of poor clergymen, with pedigrees longer than their purses, found secure and honourable service as housekeepers and ladies' maids. A new order of things had come round. The still-room[2] was no longer a safe retreat to decayed gentlewomen. A love of show kept pace with the desire of knowledge. A profligate adept in confectionary was preferred before a respectable woman, who knew the business of preserving order and decency better than the mysteries of the stew-pan and the ice-pail.[3]

---

1 An ell-wand is a measuring stick approximately 45 inches long. It derives from "ell," a measuring unit used by tailors to measure textiles. A steelyard is a balance that uses a sliding weight along a calibrated arm to indicate weight.

2 A housekeeper's storeroom.

3 Materials needed to make confectionaries.

The policy of the world is to take advantage of want. It became apparent that a whole family of daughters might be taught by one of these single women, struggling for bread, for less than it formerly cost to send one girl to school. Where competition was so great, there was no difficulty in driving a bargain. The means of instruction might be had so cheaply, that the grocer's daughters could be taught to read Paul and Virginia in the original tongue, and to strum the Fall of Paris.[1] In process of time, therefore, a governess became a necessary appanage in every family.

Whether it be right or wrong, as a general rule, for mothers to delegate their most sacred trust to hired strangers, we are not here to discuss. The fact exists. Is the system carried out fairly for all parties? Is there any question astir as to its abuse? Philanthropic eyes are scanning many social evils. Is it yet considered how far a whole race of women are dragging out weary lives under a mass of trials, the detail of which would fill a "blue book"[2] by themselves? True, if the case were known, "a thousand voices" would be "uplifted."[3] The miseries of the governess may even swell that sickening clamour about the "rights of women," which would never have been raised had women been true to themselves. But that trite saying in this case has its point. The modern governess system is a case between woman and woman. Before one sex demands its due from the other, let it be just to itself.

[...]

One cannot conceive of a greater anomaly than that which makes a woman responsible for children, and their exemplar in all things, whose mother treats her as if she were unfit to associate with herself and her guests. Children, who only look to the outside of things, must draw the inference that their governess is a mere machine for teaching. To their eyes, she appears wholly cut off from the links in their chain of sympathies. She, with all the exuberance of a youthful heart,

---

1 Jacques-Henri Bernardin de Saint-Pierre's (1737–1814) *Paul et Virginie*, a sentimental French novel published in 1788. "The Fall of Paris" most likely refers to the popular song, also known as "The Surrender of Paris" or "The Downfall of Paris," composed by Louis Jansen (b. 1774).

2 A Parliamentary report.

3 Referring to the article's epigraph from George Sand's (1804–76) *Lettres à Marcie* (1837): "Society is full of abuses. Women complain of being brutally enslaved, badly brought up, badly educated, badly treated, and badly defended. All this is, unfortunately, true. These complaints are just, and do not doubt but that before long a thousand voices will be uplifted to remedy the evil."

fresh from the warmth and common interests of a family, is suddenly thrust into a post whose conscientious fulfilment requires a discretion and reticence not natural to youth. New difficulties and responsibilities meet her every day; she is hourly tried by all those childish follies and perversities which need a mother's instinctive love to make them tolerable; yet a forbearance and spring of spirits is claimed from the stranger, in spite of the frets she endures, which He who made the heart knew that maternal affection only could supply, under the perpetual contradictions of wilful childhood. This strength of instinct has been given to every mother. It enables her to walk lightly under a load which, without it, she could not sustain. But should not women think twice, before they expect from strangers who have not even the natural affection of kindred, a mother's conduct to their children? Day by day the governess is worn by the disappointments the most promising child must inflict upon its teacher; but to whom can she, in her weariness, turn for sympathy? Not one mother in a thousand can bear to hear her child's faults spoken of by a third person, however quick-sighted she is to them herself, without some resentment towards the speaker. A very young woman would probably fear to venture on such delicate ground with the parents.

If she is indiscreet, she writes to her family about her pupils, and is taught hereafter by bitter experience the fruits of incaution; some, perhaps, go on all their lives betraying a holy trust. The lips of a conscientious teacher would be sealed, by the awe of looking in upon a child's soul and seeing all its struggles. For no relief to herself could she dare to expose to others what she has learned by a trust implicit as that placed in a confessor. She must live daily amidst the trials of a home without its blessings; she must bear about on her heart the sins she witnesses and the responsibilities that crush her; without any consent of her will, she is made the *confidante* of many family secrets; she must live in a familiar circle as if her eyes did not perceive the tokens of bitterness; she must appear not to hear sharp sayings and *mal-à-propos*[1] speeches; kindly words of courtesy must be always on her lips; she must be ever on her guard; let her relax her self-restraint for one moment, and who shall say what mischief and misery might ensue to all from one heedless expression of hers? Wholesome discipline, no doubt! It were well, perhaps, if it were made the groundwork of all home intercourse; but who amongst the young, unaided and without counsel, is sufficient for these things? Is not caution the fruit of experience? Ay, and these young creatures, if they have high moral principles, learn enough bitter experience in a year to give them the sorrows of maturity, without its strength and safety.

---

1 Inappropriate (French).

[...]

This brings us to the *£. s. d.*[1] part of the business. Very shameful instances of insufficient payment for hard service might be adduced. We rather wish, by taking the average, to secure ourselves from the charge of exaggeration. Every one is too willing to silence his own conscience by impeaching his neighbour's. We hope we may be deemed to strike the mean, if we fix the usual rate of payment at 35*l.* per annum. We believe that where there is one at 40*l.* there are two at 30*l.* Many receive much higher salaries. 100*l.* per annum may be the maximum. We know that 12*l.* per annum has been offered and accepted.

[...]

Every one who has the power ought to be able, through his industry, to maintain himself. We have sometimes been astonished at comparing the qualifications required in letters of inquiry touching governesses with the remuneration offered,—such a catalogue of literary, ornamental, and moral acquirements as one would think no ordinary mortal would lay claim to; and all these demands on body and mind to be paid by a paltry 40*l.* a year! It is not a fair interest upon the capital invested in the girl's education. One cannot learn French, German, Italian, Latin, music, dancing, and drawing, to say nothing of history, globes, and arithmetic, for nothing. It may be asked, Why does the girl close with such an offer? Let the old proverb reply, "Better half a loaf than no bread." The market is over-stocked; governesses are much at a discount. Many ladies would not dare to treat their maids as they behave to the teacher of their children. Why? The maid has a broad field before her; she can afford to turn upon her mistress. The governess must endure all things, or perish. A low marriage or a slow death are her only loopholes of escape. Oh, shame on us who make a gain of the pressing miseries of others![2]

---

1 Symbols for British pounds, shillings, and pence.

2 According to Kathryn Hughes, "between 1830 and 1890 nearly all governesses earned between £20 and £100, with the vast majority receiving between £35 and £80" (*The Victorian Governess* [London and Rio Grande, OH: Hambledon P, 1993], 155). Although governesses did not have to pay room and board, they were required to spend money on new clothing in order to maintain a respectable appearance, which often took about half of an already small salary. Governesses frequently had to pay for books, sheet music, and art supplies out of their salaries, and many supported dependent family members. These continuing expenses meant that governesses saved little to no money and remained at the bottom of the pay scale compared to women who worked in service, shops, or factories.

[...]

The most direct remedy for all these evils would appear to be to induce governesses to measure themselves by a higher rule. If they were raised in their own eyes, they would be more looked up to by others. In order to this, it is necessary that they should better understand the nature of their calling. If they saw more clearly the end of their vocation, and strove to fulfil it, they would make the way plainer for their successors. Pupils who have been carefully trained in habits of self-culture, and with a right appreciation of education, will, in their turn, be better able to do the like office to their children. If circumstances oblige such pupils hereafter to hire instructors for their families, we may be sure that such mothers will have a truer sympathy, and would more justly value the governesses of their children, than those who have been brought up by women, who, whilst they taught, despised themselves for teaching. It is not too much to say, that governesses of the present day have it in their power to remedy the abuse of the system under which they groan far more than their superiors can do. They can train the mother that will be, to teach her own child, not yet in existence. But this working for the future may be too much to be expected from the people of to-day.

There are other ways, more immediate in their result, of ameliorating the condition of female teachers. The market is glutted. If the supply were lessened, the demand would be greater. Let women labour in other fields, and thus diminish the superabundant stock of teachers. New tracks are beginning to open. The female school of design for the improvement of manufactures might profitably occupy much time and skill, now wasted in copying monstrous Arabs and gaudy Corsairs.[1] There are many women as capable of discharging the offices of clerk and book-keeper as men; besides, the will finds the way. What may not determined perseverance achieve? If, by such diversion, the services of the remaining governesses were enhanced in worth, they would necessarily fetch a higher price.

[...]

A system which suffered nature to work we may be sure would produce healthier results, there would be more startling differences between woman and woman. The quick and the dull, the volatile and

---

1 Arabs and corsairs (pirates or privateers operating along the Barbary Coast) were considered mysterious, romantic outsiders and bandits. They became popular in Britain (especially among young women) after the publication of Lord Byron's (1788–1824) *The Corsair* (1814).

the reflecting, would furnish contrasts to each other. What a cheering prospect! We may hope again to see some originality of character, some of the freshness and spirit of our grandmothers, tempered to more feminine softness by the increase of refinement. All the sisters in one family will not be cast in one type. They will not all talk out of the same books, sport the same opinions, play the same pieces. Welcome the day when we may quote again the old saw, "Many men, many minds," and include woman in the variety! Such free growth of mind and body would much conduce to those habits of exertion we have hitherto advocated. Let any woman try the interest of cutting out a line for herself, fitting herself for it, gaining day by day upon her object. She will never again be content with drawing-room idleness. She will find herself wonderfully relieved from all fears of being left upon the shelf. Or if she marry, her husband will not find her a less useful wife, a less pleasant companion, from her having been accustomed to make and execute plans of action.

We live in a hard, work-a-day world. Women of to-day, in as far as they are self-dependent, will win its respect and their own repose. Yet a few words more. *Self-dependence* is not *independence*; strength and softness are not incompatible with each other. If women who have vigorously used their faculties have thereby lost their distinctive womanly graces, it is not that such activity must needs foster a masculine temper. There have hitherto been only rare instances of women who dare to use their energies, except as wives and mothers. Singularity of position is apt to lead to eccentricity of conduct. But let the world's eye be used to contemplate female labour, and the single woman will toil in her chosen path with as much of womanly reserve and gentleness as marks the matron in her sphere of activity.

2. From Sarah Lewis, "On the Social Position of Governesses," *Fraser's Magazine* (April 1848): 411–14

The following remarks, on a subject of some public importance, were originally called forth by an application from a distinguished friend of the writer, who requested assistance for the bazar about to be held in aid of the "Governesses' Benevolent Institution." Some friends to whom they were communicated urged their publication, as placing the claims of governesses on grounds more consistent with their truth and value, than public opinion, or even public benevolence, has yet attained to respecting that important body. It is hoped that they may have some interest from the novelty, and some weight from the fact, of their coming from one *within*, and not *without* the "pale."

[...]

It is too true that governesses can rarely provide for old age or contingencies. But why? Because the emolument received by governesses (however superior) is not sufficient to enable a person, required to keep up the appearance of a gentlewoman, to do so—because the general notions on this subject are notoriously such, as to have been made the subject of more than one popular burlesque! The salary of a first-rate governess is scarcely more than the interest of money which her education *ought* to have cost; and those of all under "first-rate" are not more than is given to the upper servants of good families. The profession of a private governess is the only profession which offers no premium to distinguished abilities, and we see the results, unhappily, every day. Would it not be better to pay governesses a little more, and to pity them a little less? The prejudices which would degrade, and the injustice which inadequately remunerates, the members of an honourable and useful profession, are ill compensated by a tardy and patronising compassion. The writer knows not how the members of her profession feel *generally*, but, for her own part, she would prefer having recourse to that legal provision which the laws of her country allow all to claim,—to receiving in the form of *alms* that which had been denied in the form of *wages*. Nor can it be wondered at if the high-minded amongst the body should reject, rather than be grateful for, that form of compensation which arises from public charity, and is to be sued for *in formâ pauperis*.[1]

But this is not the only, nor, in the writer's opinion, the gravest, aspect of the subject. That individuals should suffer humiliation is a light thing in comparison of a great cause suffering injury.

Education is a great cause. The public think it so; they talk of it, at least, as such! The progress of society permits no one now to *say*, whatever he may *think*, that ours is a degrading occupation. We have essays on education, essays on educators; how the tone of the one and the character of the other may be raised. Can the tone of education, or the character of educators, be raised, while society continues to offer to the members of this profession for their services—the wages and social position of a domestic, and for their distresses and old age—the provision of a pauper?

[...]

The public feeling on this subject has already found representatives in two bodies,—the "Queen's College," and the "College of Precep-

1 "In the form of a pauper" (Latin legal).

tors."[1] To both—and especially to the latter, as organised by the Educational body itself—much gratitude is due for their endeavours after a great moral and national good. But the writer (with diffidence) suggests that they are both deficient in a most important respect,—viz. they are not armed with a competent and efficient weight of authority. The power needed is a power of *exclusion*,—a power which can say, "You shall not take up this vocation unless you shew testimonials of ability." No privately organised body would, or could, assume to itself the power of such exclusion; and the assumption, that the diploma granted to the capable would amount to a virtual exclusion of the incapable, seems to be based on an insufficient consideration of the peculiar difficulties of the case.

Some of these difficulties the writer (also with diffidence) ventures to suggest. It appears to her, that while the ignorant and incapable might (by accepting low salaries) evade the requisite examination, the *very superior*—those of acknowledged merit and talent—might neglect it, not from contempt, but because nothing but a Government diploma, absolutely indispensable, and giving to the educator the dignity of a recognised public functionary, could be to such persons a sufficient desideratum to induce them to submit to the ordeal of a public examination. Now these are the very persons whom it would be desirable to tempt into that profession to which society entrusts its dearest interests. It appears also to her, that no amount of fairness or impartiality could secure the members of those bodies from the suspicion of partisanship in the exercise of their self-constituted functions; and that the clamour of injustice—first raised, perhaps, by disappointed incapacity—would soon find an echo in the public mind, and nullify the benefits expected. A Government sanction, then, appears to be the principal means by which the object so laudably attempted by these bodies can be attained; and the *only* means by which full security can be given, either to the profession or to the public, that the highest of all tasks may not often be assigned to the lowest of all minds!

[...]

1 Queen's College was established in 1848 by the Governesses' Benevolent Institution for the purpose of providing additional education and training to women who, for a year, attended a series of lectures given by King's College instructors. The women could receive a certificate on one subject or a proficiency certificate in three subjects. The College of Preceptors was founded in 1846 in order to provide a more regulated and structured system of examination for educators.

If these remarks prove suggestive of any useful thoughts to the public in general, the writer will be well content; but her chief object is to rouse the attention of those of her own sex and profession, who may not yet have considered the subject in its full bearings, on their own position and interests, as well as on the public good. *To* them she looks for sympathy; *from* them must come the efforts (whether pecuniary or otherwise) that are to overcome the evils which all must deplore. Why should not the heads of prosperous and respectable ladies' schools come to the rescue of their less fortunate sisters? An annual subscription of comparatively moderate amount from all such would effect much good in this cause. To be the pensioners of a fund having (at least for its basis) a professional combination is one thing; to be the pauperised claimants of eleemosynary public charity is another. To rescue the less fortunate members of our noble common profession from so degrading a necessity would seem to be an object needing no other recommendation than its own merits. And if this appeal rouse a few thinking heads and noble hearts (there are some such amongst us) to consideration and consequent action, it will not have been made in vain.

3. From Emily Peart, *A Book for Governesses* (Edinburgh: W. Oliphant, [1868]), 9–22

From Chapter 1, "Change"

It is not specially for those who have been brought up and educated with a view to their being governesses, and who, consequently, have accepted the occupation as their natural work, that these pages have been written; they are rather intended for those who, by sudden strokes of adverse fortune, or by change in one shape or another, are brought down from ease and wealth to a state of dependence upon work for their daily bread.

Work is a noble and a glorious thing—a blessing and a boon. In one way or another, it is the happy lot of all; for rank and riches exempt no one from work of some kind. But sometimes the sudden shock, which reveals so unexpected a fact as poverty, has scarcely passed, before the truth presses on the heart and brain of the sufferer, "Henceforth, for the hitherto *unnoticed* needs of daily life, I have none but myself to look to." Imagine for a moment, cherished daughter of a happy home, what the feeling is that you have no *right* to utter the sweet words, "My home;"—imagine what it is to be away from friends, companions, the associates of your youth, to have to bear the coldness of strangers, the exactions of employers, the patronage of inferiors; to be measured exactly for how much you are worth in a business-like and financial point of view; your capabilities questioned, your acquirements displayed, your appearance criticised; your manners, your deportment, your dress commented upon; and all to be added up and decided, and their sum total to be told out[1] in £, s. d. Think of the same routine of work day by day—work, not to be rewarded by a mother's kiss, a father's smile, and the joy of the evening gathering round the family hearth,—and you will have pictured to yourself the lot of hundreds of your sisters; on many of whom it has fallen as a sudden blight. Let such remember that it is not by smothering sorrow, or by trying to keep it down, as if it did not exist, that it is to be conquered; but by bravely facing it and dealing with it. It is there in its intensity; let them realize it, and then set about the best way of bearing it.

[...]

There is an excess of sensitiveness in the feelings of a girl who has lost the shelter of a home, when she knows for the first time her position, which must be felt to be in the least understood. She is suffering, and suffering makes her weak. It is not to the *always* poor, but to the suddenly-made poor, that the slight, meant or unmeant, comes with keen meaning. In sound health you never feel a hundred influences, which in weakness and sickness affect you most painfully. Actions, which before would have passed unnoticed, are misconstrued; favours, which before would have been joyfully accepted, are now refused with a morbid shrinking; words, which before would have been unheeded, are full of new and stinging meaning; eyes washed with hot tears are quick to see things which do not really exist. The shock sustained, and the bewilderment accompanying it, absorb, and cannot but absorb, for a time, every thought and feeling; and the breaking heart finds utterance in the helpless question: "What *can* I do?" Well, then, in the first place, you can be silent; then you can be patient; and then you can be brave.

[...]

But what can you do? After questionings, and doubts, and anxieties, you come to the determination to teach, and you inquire after a situation; and here, again, you must be patient. You may have long to wait; you may have hopes of many situations, and be disappointed; you may miss one you think would have suited you, and you may at last be compelled to accept one which is not at all what you would wish; but if it come immediately before you, in the plain path of duty, take it;

---

1 Counted out.

only be sure it *is* the plain path of duty, or you cannot enter it rightly. It is very trying for some ladies to receive into their houses those whom they feel to be in a reduced position; and they naturally prefer ladies who have been educated for the work of teaching, and who have all along kept this in view. There are strong objections in the minds of some, to a lady who is compelled unexpectedly to teach, and to teach just for a living. You will find this a great obstacle to obtaining a good situation. Few would willingly receive into their homes one who is in great trouble; few especially would choose such a one as an instructress for their children, who need and *must have* a cheerful, sympathizing person with them. There is also the difficulty of properly treating any one in such a position. A lady shrinks from receiving one who will constantly be looking for attentions which she cannot give.

[...]

Expect, then, again and again to miss an opportunity, and not to obtain a situation about which you are asking. If you are in treaty for a situation, if it be possible make salary scarcely any object. You cannot command a large one, because you have had no experience. Respectability and character in those with whom you are going to reside are the chief things; make sure of these—as sure as it is possible to be, and let salary at first be quite a minor consideration. On your first situation, and what it is to you, and you to it, depend mainly the comfort and success of your future career. On no account let a higher salary influence you if other requirements are questionable; it is nothing to you *now* compared with the integrity and uprightness of your employers. You probably may have to lay aside the style of dress to which you have been accustomed, and appear as plain as is consistent with good taste. If you are a lady, you will look like one; the only thing you have now to consider is as perfect neatness and ladylike appearance as can be obtained with the strictest economy.

Be willing to be questioned,—not impertinently questioned, as to family affairs and plans; but as to everything pertaining to your new duties shrink from no questioning, painful as it may and will be. Your accomplishments are not now to be the theme of loving friends and admiring acquaintances, but the means of an honourable independence and of obtaining money. Face the real truth; they are simply to be calculated at trade value; and "the value of a thing is just as much as it will bring." Do not too confidently say you are sure you can do so and so—you are perfectly equal to *that*—you are not in the least afraid, and so forth. If you are not afraid, you ought to be with a right fear. Say simply what your education has been, what you believe you most excel in, and your determination to do your best. Far rather risk losing a good situation by stating truthfully only what you can do, than for a moment profess to do what you cannot. Strive to acquire perfect command over your feelings during the unpleasant ordeal of "inquiring after a situation." You will have many a pang to bear; mind you bear all bravely. There are those who have suffered as much as you,—those in whose memory's register the remembrance of such a time is written in burning letters. You must be content to endure many things which at first will seem strange, but which will all disappear in time. You are utterly new to your work now, and it to you. All has to be learnt. The first lessons are always the most discouraging, the most trying. Hundreds of difficulties, which now seem to you insuperable, will all in time disappear before courage, patience, and determination.

Try not to decide as to the merits of your situation until you have been in it for six months. You will give a very different verdict at the end of this time from that which you would have given at the beginning. Do not fill your letters to your friends with accounts which at the end of a year you may wish had never been written. Again and again consider you have all to learn; and the first lesson to you, as to all others, is the most difficult.

4. From *The Letters of Charlotte Brontë*, vol. 1, ed. Margaret Smith (Oxford: Clarendon, 1995), 193–94, 246–47

a. Charlotte Brontë to Ellen Nussey, 30 June 1839

[Swarcliffe]

My dearest Ellen[1]

I am writing a letter to you with pencil because I cannot just now procure ink without going into the drawing-room—where I do not wish to go. I only received your letter yesterday for we are not now residing at Stonegappe—but at Swarcliffe a summer residence of Mr Greenwood's Mrs Sidgwick's father. It is near Harrogate—& Ripon—a beautiful place in a beautiful country—rich and agricultural—

I should have written to you long since—and told you of every detail of the utterly new scene into which I have lately been cast—had I not been daily expecting a letter from yourself—and wondering and lamenting that you did not write for you will remember it was your turn. I must not bother you too much with my sorrows Ellen, of which

1 Ellen Nussey (1817–97) was a lifelong friend of Charlotte Brontë. The two met in 1831 while they were students at Roe Head School, Mirfield, West Yorkshire.

I fear you have heard an exaggerated account—if you were near me perhaps I might be tempted to tell you all—to grow egotistical and pour out the long history of a Private Governesse's trials and crosses in her first Situation—As it is I will only ask you to imagine the miseries of a reserved wretch like me—thrown at once into the midst of a large Family—proud as peacocks & wealthy as Jews—at a time when they were particularly gay—when the house was full of Company—all Strangers people whose faces I had never seen before—in this state of things having the charge given me of a set of pampered spoilt & turbulent children—whom I was expected constantly to amuse as well as instruct—I soon found that the constant demand on my stock of animal spirits reduced them to the lowest state of exhaustion—at times I felt and I suppose seemed depressed—to my astonishment I was taken to task on the subject by Mrs Sidgwick with a sternness of manner & a harshness of language scarcely credible—like a fool I cried most bitterly—I could not help it—my spirits quite failed me at first. I thought I had done my best—strained every nerve to please her—and to be treated in that way merely because I was shy—and sometimes melancholy was too bad. At first I was for giving all up and going home—But after a little reflection I determined—to summon what energy I had, and to weather the Storm. I said to myself I had never yet quitted a place without gaining a friend—Adversity is a good school—the Poor are born to labour and the Dependent to endure. I resolved to be patient—to command my feelings and to take what came—the ordeal I reflected would not last many weeks—and I trusted it would do me good—I recollected the fable of the Willow and the Oak[1]—I bent quietly and I trust now the Storm is blowing over me—Mrs Sidgwick is generally considered an agreeable woman—so she is I daresay in general Society—her health is sound—her animal spirits good—consequently she is cheerful in company—but O Ellen does this compensate for the absence of every fine feeling of every gentle—and delicate sentiment?—

She behaves somewhat more civilly to me now than she did at first—and the children are a little more manageable—but she does not know my character & she does not wish to know it. I have never had five minutes conversation with her since I came—except when she was scolding me—do not communicate the contents of this letter to any

1 Aesop's fable "The Oak and the Reed" is about an oak tree and a reed that encounter a strong storm. The oak tree, thinking its strength will allow it to prevail, stands firm and subsequently breaks in the heavy winds. The reed, unlike the tree, bends with the wind and survives. The story is used to teach the virtue of humility over pride and inspired such proverbs as "it is better to bend than to break."

one—I have no wish to be *pitied*—except by yourself—do not even chatter with Martha Taylor[1] about it—if I were talking to you I would tell you much more—but I hope my term of bondage will soon be expired—and then I can go home and you can come to see me—and I hope we shall be happy.

b. Charlotte Brontë to Ellen Nussey, 3 March 1841

[Upperwood House, Rawdon]

My dear Ellen,

I told you some time since, that I meant to get a situation, and when I said so my resolution was quite fixed. I felt that however often I was disappointed, I had no intention of relinquishing my efforts. After being severely baffled two or three times,—after a world of trouble in the way of correspondence and interviews,—I have at length succeeded, and am fairly established in my new place. It is in the family of Mr. W[hite], of U[pperwood House, Rawdon].[2]

The house is not very large, but exceedingly comfortable, and well regulated; the grounds are fine and extensive. In taking this place I have made a large sacrifice in the way of salary, in the hope of securing comfort, by which word I do not mean to express good eating and drinking, or warm fire, or a soft bed, but the society of cheerful faces, and minds and hearts not dug out of a lead-mine, or cut from a marble quarry. My salary is not really more than £16 per annum, though it is nominally £20, but the expense of washing will be deducted therefrom. My pupils are two in number, a girl of eight and a boy of six. As to my employers, you will not expect me to say much respecting their characters when I tell you that I only arrived here yesterday. I have not the faculty of telling an individual's disposition at first sight. Before I can venture to pronounce on a character, I must see it first under various lights, and from various points of view. All I can say therefore is, both Mr and Mrs W[hite] seem to me good sort of people. I have as yet had no cause to complain of want of considerateness or civility. My pupils are wild and unbroken, but apparently well disposed. I wish I may be able to say as much next time I write to you. My earnest wish and endeavour will be to please them. If I can but feel that I am giving satisfaction, and if at the same time I can keep my health, I shall, I

---

1 Martha Taylor (1819–42) was a friend and fellow schoolmate of Charlotte Brontë at Roe Head School.

2 Brontë served as governess at Upperwood House from February to December 1841. John White (c. 1790–1860) was a merchant in nearby Bradford.

hope, be moderately happy. But no one but myself can tell how hard a governess's work is to me—for no one but myself is aware how utterly averse my whole mind and nature are to the employment. Do not think that I fail to blame myself for this, or that I leave any means unemployed to conquer this feeling. Some of my greatest difficulties lie in things that would appear to you comparatively trivial. I find it so hard to repel the rude familiarity of children. I find it so difficult to ask either servants or mistress for anything I want, however much I want it. It is less pain to me to endure the greatest inconvenience than to go [into the kitchen to] request its removal. I am a fool. Heaven knows I cannot help it!

5. From Dinah Mulock Craik, *Bread upon the Waters: A Governess's Life* (London: Governesses' Benevolent Institution, 1852), 129, 130–33, 148–49

From Part 1.

To-morrow I shall remove with my brothers to a lodging, try to get daily pupils, and begin the world, with a good education, youth, health, courage, and twenty pounds a year. Not so bad!—the very thought of toil gives me strength. It is like plunging into a cold bath, after being suffocated with foul vapory steams.

A strange thought smote me just now. What will all my friends say?—what will *one friend* say, when he comes back and finds me—a daily governess?

Still, no matter—it must be.

From Part 2.

What a strange, new life is this on which I have entered so boldly! To-day, after paying my weekly rent in advance, making some slight needful purchases, and providing, much too largely I fear, for household expenses and food, I find we have exactly one sovereign to begin the world with. Well! as my clever Harry remarked, "Benjamin Franklin began with one shilling;"[1] so we are fully nineteen shillings

1 When Benjamin Franklin (1706–90) arrived in Philadelphia in 1723, he had no connections and no employment prospects. He wrote in his *Autobiography* (1791): "I was in my working dress, my best clothes being to come round by sea. I was dirty from my journey; my pockets were stuff'd out with shirts and stockings, and I knew no soul nor where to look for lodging. I was fatigued with traveling, rowing, and want of rest, I was very hungry; and my whole stock of cash consisted of a Dutch dollar, and about a shilling in copper."

the richer than that great philosopher. Nevertheless, I am glad that my teaching duties commence to-morrow, and that my first week's salary will soon be due.

(Looking back on these days, it seems to me almost a miracle that I had got this situation, the very first I applied for. It must have been some charitable soul who gave me through pity what I took as an ordinary right, not knowing how many a poor unknown, uncredentialed governess waits, hopes, doubts, gradually sinks down lower and lower, despairs, and starves.)

I have taken our lodgings where would be cheapest, and furthest away from our old neighborhood; therefore I shall have a rather long walk into town to my pupil; but exercise is good for me. The boys will be quiet at home; our old servant, who keeps these lodgings, will have an eye upon them; and I shall teach them of an evening. I began to do it to-night, but rather unsuccessfully; they have been too much excited by the change. So I took Aleck on my knee, while Henry placed himself on the other side the fire, quite man-like; and we had a serious talk about "our establishment."

[...]

I have gone through the first week of my life as a daily governess. It has been rather harder than I had thought.

I found my one pupil a very big girl, indeed almost a young woman, taller than myself and with twice as much spirit. She really frightened me, with her fierce black eyes, and her foreign manner, for she is half French. I felt myself shrinking into nothing beside her. Yet though she chattered French and German to an extent that at first alarmed me, on the score of my own acquirements, I find her lamentably ignorant in the real classic knowledge of either language; and as regards English she requires the teaching I would give to little Aleck. Nevertheless, she has such perfect self-assurance, such a strong will, such a thorough ease and independence of manner, that one requires the utmost moral courage to attempt to teach her any thing. I try to assume all my dignity, and the decision of superior years and knowledge, but yet I am only one-and-twenty, while she is near fifteen. And oh! if she did but know how dreadfully her poor little governess is at heart afraid of her!

I believed myself tolerably well-educated; surely I am, as regards classical literature. How I always reveled in Dante, and loved the only true French poet, Lamartine, and dived thirstingly into the mysteries of Goethe and Schiller:[1] yet in common conversation I find myself nonplussed continually. It is such a different matter to know a thing oneself, and to impart it to another. I ought now to go to school again, if only to learn how to teach.

There it is again in music. Friends call me a good musician (at least *some* friends did), and I know my love for it is a perfect passion: but there is a vast difference between singing for oneself, or for those whom one cares to please far better than one's self—and knocking a poor song note by note into the ear and head of a girl who has no more heart for it than, alas! her poor governess has for the teaching. I had to-day to play and sing before Thérèse's mother in proof of my acquirements. I chose a song—sang many a time to such pleasant praises! but in the singing my eyes filled with tears, and my heart sank down like lead. I failed deplorably; and I knew it. I had no business to think of such things now I am a daily governess.

Occasionally, too, I have stings of foolish pride; I had today, when Madame Giraud asked me abruptly, "if I wanted my salary?" My cheeks burned, as I said, "Yes, if she pleased," and took the gold, so much needed. I thought—if any old friends could see me then, would they scorn me? But I soon got over this wrong feeling, and walking home, enjoyed the sweetness of first earnings.

Yet at the week's end I am very tired, probably with the long daily walk and the perpetual talking. I am so glad tomorrow is Sunday!

I see clearly, we must live somewhat plainer than we do. It costs more to feed three mouths weekly than I had expected: and as for my taking the omnibus to town on wet days, as Harry insists—wise, thoughtful little man!—*that* is quite impossible; but I need not vex him by saying so.

How changed we all are in a few weeks! how it seems like an age since we "began the world!" The children have become quite used to our new ways, only, poor things! sometimes they can not understand

---

1 Dante Alighieri (1265–1321) was the famed Italian poet renowned for his influential three-part epic *The Divine Comedy*, written in the early fourteenth century. Alphonse de Lamartine (1790–1869) was a French poet and diplomat whose *Méditations Poétiques* (1820) established him as one of the pre-eminent figures of French Romantic literature. A member of the German Romantic movement, Johann Wolfgang von Goethe (1749–1832) achieved fame with his novel *The Sorrows of Young Werther* (1774) and later with his epic tragedy *Faust* (Part 1 [1808], Part 2 [1833]). Goethe's friend and collaborator Friedrich Schiller (1759–1805) is best known for dramas such as *The Robbers* (1781), the *Wallenstein* trilogy (1800), *Mary Stuart* (1801), and *Wilhelm Tell* (1804).

why they are restricted in what were once ordinary things, but have now become impracticable luxuries. Harry wants to go out always in his best jacket and French kid gloves; and Aleck still looks and longs daily for the pudding. Poor lads! it goes to my very heart sometimes.

I have not leisure to write my journal often, being every night so glad to go to bed. It is a great blessing that I have such sound, wholesome sleep, which not only refreshes me, but drowns all care for a season.

If I could only send those boys to school, even to the common school they used to attend, I would be so thankful! It is not right for them to be left alone the long, long day; and at night I am so tired, that I fear I do not teach them half carefully enough. I must try some plan or other for them.

From Part 3.

When [Sir Godfrey] said so, I smiled, and in my turn reminded him that I was still "the governess."

"Well!" he answered, "and what is more honorable than a governess, when she is a lady by birth, or at least by education, as all governesses ought to be? What more noble than a woman who devotes her whole life to the sowing of good seed, the fruitage of which she may never see? If I have a wife and children," here his eyes smiled with some dim, dawning thought, "I will teach them, that after father and mother there is no one on earth to whom they owe such reverence as to her on whom depends the formation not only of their intellect, but of their whole mind and character. But, accordingly, I will take care that this model governess is worthy of the trust—a true lady, and more, a true *woman*—in fact, just such a woman as you are yourself, Miss Lyne."

I had no answer to that. I—*his* children's governess!

Still, it gives me comfort to think he should so honor the sisterhood to which I belong—unto which I had joined myself in humiliated despair, until at last I began to wear my heavy chains as the badge of a worthy service, and to discover that every governess has it in her power to make herself, and with herself all her fraternity, reverenced and honorable in the sight of the world.

Select Bibliography and Recommended Reading

"The Author of *John Halifax*." *British Quarterly Review* 44 (July 1866): 32–58.

Ballhatchet, Kenneth. *Race, Sex and Class under the Raj: Imperial Attitudes and Policies and Their Critics, 1793–1905*. New York: St. Martin's P, 1980.

Bearce, George D. *British Attitudes towards India, 1784–1858*. Oxford: Oxford UP, 1961.

Bolt, Christine. "Race and the Victorians." *British Imperialism in the Nineteenth Century*. Ed. C.C. Eldridge. New York: St. Martin's P, 1984. 126–47.

——. *Victorian Attitudes to Race*. London: Routledge and Kegan Paul, 1971.

Bourrier, Karen. "Introduction: Rereading Dinah Mulock Craik." *Women's Writing* 20.3 (2013): 287–96.

——. "Narrating Insanity in the Letters of Thomas Mulock and Dinah Mulock Craik." *Victorian Literature and Culture* 39 (2011): 203–22.

Brandon, Ruth. *Governess: The Lives and Times of the Real Jane Eyres*. New York: Walker and Company, 2008.

Broughton, Trev, and Ruth Symes, eds. *The Governess: An Anthology*. New York: St. Martin's P, 1997.

Busia, Abena P.A. "Miscegenation as Metonymy: Sexuality and Power in the Colonial Novel." *Ethnic and Racial Studies* 9.3 (1986): 360–72.

Chandler, Robyn. "Dinah Mulock Craik: Sacrifice and the Fairy-Order." *Silent Voices: Forgotten Novels by Victorian Women Writers*. Ed. Brenda Ayres. Westport, CT, and London: Praeger, 2013. 173–201.

Colby, Robert A. *Fiction with a Purpose*. Bloomington: Indiana UP, 1967.

Collingham, E.M. *Imperial Bodies: The Physical Experience of the Raj, c. 1800–1947*. Cambridge: Polity, 2001.

Craik, Dinah Mulock. *Bread upon the Waters: A Governess's Life*. London: Governesses' Benevolent Institution, 1852.

——. "Concerning Men, By a Woman." *Cornhill Magazine* 9 (October 1887): 368–77.

——. *Olive*. 1850. Oxford Popular Fiction Series. Intro. Cora Kaplan. Oxford and New York: Oxford UP, 1996.

———. *A Woman's Thoughts about Women*. London: Hurst and Blackett, 1858.
Dalrymple, William. *White Mughals: Love and Betrayal in Eighteenth-Century India*. London: HarperCollins, 2002.
Darby, Phillip. *The Fiction of Imperialism: Reading between International Relations and Postcolonialism*. London and Washington, DC: Cassell, 1998.
David, Deirdre. *Rule Britannia: Women, Empire, and Victorian Writing*. Ithaca, NY, and London: Cornell UP, 1995.
D'Cruz, Glenn. *Midnight's Orphans: Anglo-Indians in Post/colonial Literature*. Bern and New York: Peter Lang, 2006.
Ella. "Miss Muloch (Mrs. Craik)." *The Victoria Magazine* 28 (April 1877): 479–83.
Ellis, Sarah. *The Women of England: Their Social Duties and Domestic Habits*. 1839. London: Fisher, Son, and Co., 1845.
Ellis, Stewart Marsh. "Dinah Maria Mulock (Mrs. Craik)." *Bookman* 70 (April 1926): 1–5.
Foster, Shirley. *Victorian Women's Fiction: Marriage, Freedom and the Individual*. London and Sydney: Croom Helm, 1985.
Ghosh, Durba. *Sex and the Family in Colonial India: The Making of Empire*. Cambridge and New York: Cambridge UP, 2006.
Greenberger, Allen J. *The British Image of India: A Study of the Literature of Imperialism, 1880–1960*. London and New York: Oxford UP, 1969.
Grimshaw, Allen D. "The Anglo-Indian Community: The Integration of a Marginal Group." *The Journal of Asian Studies* 18.2 (February 1959): 227–40.
Gupta, Brijen K. *India in English Fiction, 1800–1970: An Annotated Bibliography*. Metuchen, NJ: Scarecrow P, 1973.
"Half-Castes." *Minutes of Evidence Taken before the Select Committee on the Affairs of the East India Company*. House of Commons. 16 August 1832. 300–01.
Hall, Catherine. *White, Male and Middle Class: Explorations in Feminism and History*. New York: Routledge, 1992.
Hamilton, M. [Mary Churchill Luck]. *Poor Elisabeth*. London: Hurst and Blackett, 1901.
Hawes, Christopher J. *Poor Relations: The Making of a Eurasian Community in British India, 1773–1833*. Richmond, UK: Curzon, 1996.
Hill, Bridget. *Women Alone: Spinsters in England, 1660–1850*. New Haven, CT, and London: Yale UP, 2001.
"Hints on the Modern Governess System." *Fraser's Magazine* 30 (November 1844): 571–83.
Hockley, William Browne. "The Half-Caste Daughter." *The Widow of*

Calcutta; The Half-Caste Daughter; and Other Sketches. Vol. 2. London: D.N. Carvalho, 1841. 182–205.
Howe, Susanne. *Novels of Empire*. New York: Columbia UP, 1949.
Hughes, Kathryn. *The Victorian Governess*. London and Rio Grande, OH: Hambledon P, 1993.
Hutton, R.H. "Novels by the Authoress of 'John Halifax.'" *North British Review* 29 (1858): 466–81.
Hyam, Ronald. *Empire and Sexuality: The British Experience*. Manchester and New York: Manchester UP, 1990.
Jameson, Anna. *The Relative Social Position of Mothers and Governesses*. London, 1846.
Kapila, Shuchi. *Educating Seeta: The Anglo-Indian Family Romance and the Poetics of Indirect Rule*. Columbus: Ohio State UP, 2010.
Kaplan, Cora. "Imagining Empire: History, Fantasy and Literature." *At Home with the Empire: Metropolitan Culture and the Imperial World*. Ed. Catherine Hall and Sonya O. Rose. Cambridge: Cambridge UP, 2006. 191–211.
Kincaid, Dennis. *British Social Life in India, 1608–1937*. London: Routledge, 1938.
"The Lady Novelists of Great Britain." *Gentlemen's Magazine* 40 (July 1853): 18–25.
Lahiri, Shompa. *Indians in Britain: Anglo-Indian Encounters, Race and Identity, 1880–1930*. London and Portland, OR: Frank Cass, 2000.
Lecaros, Cecilia Wadsö. *The Victorian Governess Novel*. Lund, Sweden: Lund UP, 2001.
——. "The Victorian Heroine Goes A-Governessing." *Silent Voices: Forgotten Novels by Victorian Women Writers*. Ed. Brenda Ayres. Westport, CT, and London: Praeger, 2013. 27–56.
Levine, Philippa, ed. *Gender and Empire*. New York and Oxford: Oxford UP, 2004.
Lewis, Sarah. "On the Social Position of Governesses." *Fraser's Magazine* 37 (April 1848): 411–14.
MacMillan, Margaret. *Women of the Raj*. New York: Thames and Hudson, 1988.
Malchow, H.L. *Gothic Images of Race in Nineteenth-Century Britain*. Stanford, CA: Stanford UP, 1996.
Mascarenhas, Kiran. "*The Half-Caste*: A Half-Told Tale." *Women's Writing* 20.3 (2013): 344–57.
Maurice, Mary. *Governess Life: Its Trials, Duties, and Encouragements*. London: John W. Parker, 1849.
Maxwell, Helen Blackmar. *The Way of Fire*. New York: Dodd, Mead and Company, 1897.

Meyer, Susan. *Imperialism at Home: Race and Victorian Women's Fiction*. Ithaca, NY: Cornell UP, 1996.

Mitchell, Sally. "Afterword: Dinah Mulock Craik for the Twenty-First Century." *Women's Writing* 20.3 (2013): 404–12.

——. *Dinah Mulock Craik*. Boston: Twayne, 1983.

——. *The Fallen Angel: Chastity, Class, and Women's Reading, 1835–1880*. Bowling Green, OH: Bowling Green U Popular P, 1981.

Moore, Rory. "A Mediated Intimacy: Dinah Mulock Craik and Celebrity Culture." *Women's Writing* 20.3 (2013): 387–403.

Moore-Gilbert, Bart, ed. *Writing India, 1757–1990: The Literature of British India*. Manchester and New York: Manchester UP, 1996.

Morey, Peter. *Fictions of India: Narrative and Power*. Edinburgh: Edinburgh UP, 2000.

Nair, Janaki. "Uncovering the Zenana: Visions of Indian Womanhood in Englishwomen's Writings, 1813–1940." *Journal of Women's History* 2.1 (Spring 1990): 8–34.

Oliphant, Margaret. "Mrs. Craik." *Macmillan's Magazine* 57 (December 1887): 81–85.

"On the Policy of the British Government towards the Indo-Britons." *Asiatic Journal* 20 (September 1825): 305–08.

Parr, Louisa. "Dinah Mulock (Mrs. Craik)." *Women Novelists of Queen Victoria's Reign*. London: Hurst and Blackett, 1897. 219–48.

Paxton, Nancy L. *Writing under the Raj: Gender, Race, and Rape in the British Colonial Imagination, 1830–1947*. New Brunswick, NJ, and London: Rutgers UP, 1999.

Peart, Emily. *A Book for Governesses*. Edinburgh: William Oliphant, [1868].

Penny, Fanny Emily. *Caste and Creed*. 2 vols. London: F.V. White, 1890.

Perera, Suvendrini. *Reaches of Empire: The English Novel from Edgeworth to Dickens*. New York: Columbia UP, 1991.

Peterson, Jeanne M. "The Victorian Governess: Status Incongruence in Family and Society." *Suffer and Be Still: Women in the Victorian Age*. Ed. Martha Vicinus. Bloomington: Indiana UP, 1973. 3–19.

Poovey, Mary. *Uneven Developments: The Ideological Work of Gender in Mid-Victorian England*. Chicago: U of Chicago P, 1988.

Rowe, A.D. *Every-day Life in India*. New York: American Tract Society, 1881.

Roye, Susmita, and Rajeshwar Mittapalli, eds. *The Male Empire under the Female Gaze: The British Raj and the Memsahib*. Amherst, NY: Cambria, 2013.

Sandberg, Graham. "Our Outcast Cousins in India." *Contemporary Review* 61 (June 1892): 880–99.

Sen, Indrani. *Memsahib's Writings: Colonial Narratives on Indian Women*. New Delhi: Orient Longman, 2008.
——. *Woman and Empire: Representations in the Writings of British India, 1858–1900*. Hyderabad: Orient Longman, 2002.
Sharpe, Jenny. *Allegories of Empire: The Figure of the Woman in the Colonial Text*. Minneapolis and London: U of Minnesota P, 1993.
Showalter, Elaine. "Dinah Mulock Craik and the Tactics of Sentiment: A Case Study in Victorian Female Authorship." *Feminist Studies* 2 (1975): 5–23.
——. *A Literature of Their Own: British Women Novelists from Brontë to Lessing*. Princeton, NJ: Princeton UP, 1977.
Smith, Margaret, ed. *The Letters of Charlotte Brontë*. Vol. 1. Oxford: Clarendon, 1995.
Speid, Mrs. John B. *Our Last Years in India*. London: Smith, Elder, 1862.
Suleri, Sara. *The Rhetoric of English India*. Chicago and London: U of Chicago P, 1992.
Taylor, [Philip] Meadows. *Seeta*. 1872. London: C. Kegan Paul, 1880.
Trivedi, Harish. *Colonial Transactions: English Literature and India*. Manchester and New York: Manchester UP, 1995.
West, Katharine. *Chapter of Governesses: A Study of the Governess in English Fiction, 1800–1949*. London: Cohen & West, 1949.
Young, Robert J.C. *Colonial Desire: Hybridity in Theory, Culture and Race*. London: Routledge, 1995.

From the Publisher

A name never says it all, but the word "Broadview" expresses a good deal of the philosophy behind our company. We are open to a broad range of academic approaches and political viewpoints. We pay attention to the broad impact book publishing and book printing has in the wider world; we began using recycled stock more than a decade ago, and for some years now we have used 100% recycled paper for most titles. Our publishing program is internationally oriented and broad-ranging. Our individual titles often appeal to a broad readership too; many are of interest as much to general readers as to academics and students.

Founded in 1985, Broadview remains a fully independent company owned by its shareholders—not an imprint or subsidiary of a larger multinational.

For the most accurate information on our books (including information on pricing, editions, and formats) please visit our website at www.broadviewpress.com. Our print books and ebooks are also available for sale on our site.

On the Broadview website we also offer several goods that are not books—among them the Broadview coffee mug, the Broadview beer stein (inscribed with a line from Geoffrey Chaucer's *Canterbury Tales*), the Broadview fridge magnets (your choice of philosophical or literary), and a range of T-shirts (made from combinations of hemp, bamboo, and/or high-quality pima cotton, with no child labor, sweatshop labor, or environmental degradation involved in their manufacture).

All these goods are available through the "merchandise" section of the Broadview website. When you buy Broadview goods you can support other goods too.

broadview press
www.broadviewpress.com

The interior of this book is printed on 100% recycled paper.